Little Goody Two-Shoes

by

John Newbery

*with a preface
for the Garland edition by*

Michael H. Platt

The Fairing

by

John Newbery

*with a preface
for the Garland edition by*

Brian Alderson

Garland Publishing, Inc.,

New York & London
1977

J
N

Library of Congress Cataloging in Publication Data

Goody Two Shoes.
   The history of Little Goody Two-Shoes.

   (Classics of children's literature, 1621-1932)
   The 1st work has also been attributed to O. Goldsmith
and G. Jones; attribution of the 2d work to J. Newbery is
conjectural.
   Reprint of the 1765 ed. of the 1st work, printed for
J. Newbery, London, and of the 1768 ed. of the 2d work,
printed for Newbery and Carnan, London.
   Includes bibliographical references.
   SUMMARY: In the first of these two books an orphan
girl grows up to become a wise and virtuous schoolmistress
and the second offers a series of loosely connected tales
set within the framework of a visit to the fair and
including "Puss in Boots" and "Dick Whittington."
   [1. Conduct of life--Fiction. 2. Short stories]
I. Newbery, John, 1713-1767. II. Goldsmith, Oliver,
1728-1774. III. Jones, Giles, fl. 1765. IV. The Fairing. 1977. V. Title. VI. Series.
PZ6.G639H27   [Fic]   75-32141
ISBN 0-8240-2257-2

Printed in the United States of America

The History of
Little Goody Two-Shoes

Bibliographical note:

This facsimile has been
made from a copy in
The British Library
(C.180.a.3)

A Garland Series

Classics of Children's Literature 1621-1932

A collection of 117 titles
reprinted in photo-facsimile
in 73 volumes

Selected and arranged by
Alison Lurie
and
Justin G. Schiller

THE HISTORY OF
LITTLE GOODY TWO-SHOES

Selected Bibliography:

By Justin G. Schiller

The History of Little Goody Two-Shoes; otherwise called, Mrs. Margery Two-Shoes. London 1765. Reprinted many times, including "new edition, corrected," 1766; third edition, 1766; fourth, 1767; fifth, 1768, 1770, 1772; seventh, 1774, 1775, 1777, 1780, 1783; etc.

The History of Little Goody Two-Shoes; Otherwise called, Mrs. Margery Two-Shoes. First American edition, New York: H[ugh] Gaine, 1775. Reprinted, Boston 1783; Philadelphia 1787; Worcester 1787; Philadelphia 1793; Wilmington [Delaware] 1793; etc.

The History of Goody Two-Shoes, and the Adventures of Tommy Two-Shoes [edited by William Godwin]. London: Tabart, 1804. This includes three hand-colored copper engravings. It was also anthologized by the publisher in his four-volume *Collection of Popular Stories for the Nursery: newly trans-*

Notes

1. The book was also frequently imitated; a prominent example is a volume printed by another famous eighteenth-century bookseller, John Marshall, entitled *Entertaining History of Little Goody Goose-Cap*.

2. Charles Welsh in his introduction to the facsimile reprint of the third edition in 1881 comes down strongly in favor of Goldsmith.

3. See pages 33, 61, and 67.

MICHAEL H. PLATT has been collecting rare books and first editions since 1964 and spends most of his spare time in restoring and repairing fragile bindings on old children's books. He lives in London with his wife and two children, all of whom share his taste for historical juvenile literature.

called Jones and that at the end Margery Two-Shoes becomes Lady Jones. Giles Jones' grandson, John Winter Jones, was a former principal librarian at the British Museum, and it is perhaps not coincidental that the book is attributed to Giles Jones in the British Museum catalogue.

A third possibility is that Newbery himself was the author of *Goody Two-Shoes*. Several of his other publications are advertised within the book,[3] and there is also a plug for his thriving patent medicine business. Goody Two-Shoes' father dies of a fever "in a place where Dr. James's Powder was not to be had," and a list of the medicines sold by Newbery, including the famous Dr. James's Fever Powder, appears at the end of the book.

Today, according to Harvey Darton, *Goody Two-Shoes* is "utterly dead" as a children's book. But as a piece of social history and a milestone in the history of juvenile literature, it remains one of the most important works ever published in its field.

Michael H. Platt, B.D.S.

cheaper and more acceptable to contemporary parents.[1] Part of its popularity resulted from its being one of the first and most famous moral tales for children: a story in which virtue is not only its own reward but also inevitably brings material and social benefits—a theme that persists in children's literature even to this day.

The authorship of *Goody Two-Shoes* has remained a mystery. Newbery employed many of the best writers of his time, including Dr. Johnson, Smollett, and Christopher Smart—as well as Oliver Goldsmith, to whom *Goody Two-Shoes* has sometimes been attributed.[2] Goldsmith's background and education were similar to that of the author of the Introduction to *Goody Two-Shoes*, and the attack on the cruelty and injustice of rural evictions recalls Goldsmith's poem "The Deserted Village."

Another possible author is Giles Jones, one of the two brothers, Giles and Griffiths Jones, who did much hackwork for Newbery and wrote many tales for his *Lilliputian Magazine*, among them "Giles Gingerbread" and "Tommy Trip." Some scholars include *Goody Two-Shoes* among these tales. It has been pointed out that one of the prominent families in the book is

PREFACE

Mr. Newbery's little books for the children and youth of these kingdoms and the colonies.

John Newbery charged sixpence for this story of a penniless orphan girl, Margery Meanwell, who through hard work and self-education rises to be first an elementary-school teacher and then the wife of a prosperous squire. It found immediate favor with readers and remained in print for over one hundred and fifty years. Copies of Newbery's edition reached America by 1775, and in 1787 the Worcester publisher Isaiah Thomas, who has been called the American John Newbery, printed another edition with new woodcuts based on the London original.

The 1765 Newbery version of *Goody Two-Shoes*, reproduced here, contains many extraneous episodes, including an appendix describing the adventures of Margery's brother Tommy and relating other anecdotes. For about fifty years the book was reprinted in its entirety, but from the beginning of the nineteenth century it was usually edited and abridged and brought out in chapbook form, making it both

Preface

English children's literature, in the sense of works written specifically for a juvenile audience and intended to amuse as well as to instruct, began with the eighteenth-century London publisher John Newbery (1713-1767). His first juvenile, *A Little Pretty Pocket Book*, appeared in 1744; his most famous, *The History of Little Goody Two-Shoes*, was published at the end of his career, twenty years later. It was announced in *The London Chronicle* for 27-29 December 1764 along with a half-dozen other new titles, as follows:

> We are also desired to give notice that there is in the Press and speedily will be published either by subscription or otherwise as the Public shall please to determine 'The History of Little Goody Two-Shoes' otherwise called 'Mrs. Margery Two-Shoes.' Presented and sold at the Bible and Sun in Saint Paul's Churchyard where may be had all

THE
HISTORY

OF

Little GOODY TWO-SHOES;

Otherwise called,

Mrs. MARGERY TWO-SHOES.

WITH

The Means by which she acquired her
Learning and Wisdom, and in consequence thereof her Estate; set forth
at large for the Benefit of those,

Who from a State of Rags and Care,
And having Shoes but half a Pair;
Their Fortune and their Fame would fix,
And gallop in a Coach and Six.

See the Original Manuscript in the *Vatican*
at *Rome*, and the Cuts by *Michael Angelo*.
Illustrated with the Comments of our
great modern Critics.

LONDON:
Printed for J. NEWBERY, at the *Bible* and
Sun in St. *Paul's Church-yard*, 1765.
[Price Six-Pence.]

BIBLIOGRAPHY

lated and revised, from the French, Italian, and old English writers issued this same year.

A History of Goody Two-Shoes' Birthday in Verse. London 1809. This is an imitation of Roscoe's *Butterfly's Ball & Grasshopper's Feast* and otherwise bears no relationship to the Newbery text.

The Modern Goody Two-Shoes, exemplifying the Good Consequences of Early Attention to Learning and Virtue [edited] by Mary Belson [Elliott]. London 1815.

Goody Two-Shoes, or the History of Little Margery Meanwell in Rhyme. London 1825.

Selected References:

Welsh, Charles. *A Bookseller of the Last Century being some account of John Newbery, and of the books he published*. London 1885. See also the introduction by Charles Welsh to his facsimile reprint of the third edition *History of Little Goody Two-Shoes*, London 1881.

SELECTED REFERENCES

Barry, Florence V. *A Century of Children's Books*. London 1922, pp. 67-76.

Darton, F. J. Harvey. *Children's Books in England*. Cambridge 1932, pp. 130-135.

Stone, Wilbur Macey. *The History of Little Goody Two-Shoes. An Essay and a List of Editions*. Worcester 1940 (reprinted from *The Proceedings of the American Antiquarian Society*, October 1939).

Roberts, R. J. "The 1765 Edition of Goody Two-Shoes," *British Museum Quarterly* 29 (Summer 1965): 67-70.

Thwaite, M. F. *From Primer to Pleasure*. London 1965.

Roscoe, Sydney. *John Newbery and His Successors 1740-1814*. London 1973, J167.

Little Goody Two-Shoes

TO ALL

Young Gentlemen and Ladies,

Who are good, or intend to be good,

This B O O K

Is inscribed by

Their old Friend

In St. Paul's Church-Yard.

The

The Renowned

HISTORY

O F

Little Goody Two-Shoes;

Commonly called,

Old Goody Two-Shoes.

PART I.

INTRODUCTION. By the Editor.

ALL the World muſt allow, that *Two Shoes* was not her real Name. No; her Father's Name was *Meanwell*; and he was for many Years a conſiderable Farmer in the Pariſh where *Margery* was born; but by the Misfortunes

Misfortunes which he met with in Business, and the wicked Persecutions of Sir *Timothy Gripe*, and an overgrown Farmer called *Graspall*, he was effectually ruined.

The Case was thus. The Parish of *Mouldwell* where they lived, had for many Ages been let by the Lord of the Manor into twelve different Farms, in which the Tenants lived comfortably, brought up large Families, and carefully supported the poor People who laboured for them; until the Estate by Marriage and by Death came into the Hands of Sir *Timothy.*

This Gentleman, who loved himself better than all his Neighbours, thought it less Trouble to write one Receipt for his Rent than twelve, and Farmer *Graspall* offering to take all the Farms as the Leases expired, Sir *Timothy* agreed with him, and in Process of

Time he was possessed of every Farm,
but that occupied by little *Margery*'s
Father; which he also wanted; for as
Mr. *Meanwell* was a charitable good
Man, he stood up for the Poor at the
Parish Meetings, and was unwilling to
have them oppressed by Sir *Timothy*,
and this avaricious Farmer.--Judge, oh
kind, humane and courteous Reader,
what a terrible Situation the Poor
must be in, when this covetous Man
was perpetual Overseer, and every
Thing for their Maintenance was
drawn from his hard Heart and cruel
Hand. But he was not only perpetual Overseer, but perpetual Church-
warden; and judge, oh ye Christi-
ans, what State the Church must be
in, when supported by a Man without Religion or Virtue. He was also
perpetual Surveyor of the Highways,
and what Sort of Roads he kept up
for

for the Convenience of Travellers, those best know who have had the Misfortune to be obliged to pass through that Parish.---Complaints indeed were made, but to what Purpose are Complaints, when brought against a Man, who can hunt, drink and smoak with the Lord of the Manor, who is also the Justice of Peace?

The Opposition which little *Margery*'s Father made to this Man's Tyranny gave Offence to Sir *Timothy*, who endeavoured to force him out of his Farm; and to oblige him to throw up the Lease, ordered both a Brick Kiln and a Dog-kennel to be erected in the Farmer's Orchard. This was contrary to Law, and a Suit was commenced, in which *Margery*'s Father got the better. The same Offence was again committed three different Times, and as many Actions brought,

A 4

in all of which the Farmer had a
Verdict and Costs paid him ; but
notwithstanding these Advantages,
the Law was so expensive, that he
was ruined in the Contest, and obliged to give up all he had to his
Creditors ; which effectually answered the Purpose of Sir *Timothy*, who
erected those Nuisances in the Farmer's Orchard with that Intention
only. Ah, my dear Reader, we brag
of Liberty, and boast of our Laws ;
but the Blessings of the one, and the
Protection of the other, seldom fall to
the Lot of the Poor ; and especially
when a rich Man is their Adversary.
How, in the Name of Goodness, can
a poor Wretch obtain Redress, when
thirty Pounds are insufficient to try
his Cause? Where is he to find Money to fee Council, or how can he
plead his Cause himself (even if he
was

was permitted) when our Laws are
fo obfcure, and fo multiplied, that an
Abridgment of them cannot be con-
tained in fifty Volumes in Folio?

As foon as Mr. *Meanwell* had called
together his Creditors, Sir *Timothy*
feized for a Year's Rent, and turned
the Farmer, his Wife, little *Margery*,
and her Brother out of Doors, without any of the Neceffaries of Life to
fupport them.

This

This elated the Heart of Mr. *Graspall*, this crowned his Hopes, and filled the Measure of his Iniquity; for besides gratifying his Revenge, this Man's Overthrow gave him the sole Dominion of the Poor, whom he depressed and abused in a Manner too horrible to mention.

Margery's Father flew into another Parish for Succour, and all those who were able to move left their Dwellings and sought Employment elsewhere, as they found it would be impossible to live under the Tyranny of two such People. The very old, the very lame and the blind were obliged to stay behind, and whether they were starved, or what became of them, History does not say; but the Character of the great Sir *Timothy*, and his avaricious Tenant, were so infamous, that nobody would work for them by the Day, and

Servants

Servants were afraid to engage themselves by the Year, left any unfore-
seen Accident should leave them Pa-
rishioners in a Place, where they knew
they must perish miserably; so that
great Part of the Land lay untilled
for some Years, which was deemed a
just Reward for such diabolical Proceedings.

But what, says the Reader, can occasion all this? Do you intend this
for Children, Mr. NEWBERY? Why,
do you suppose this is written by Mr.
NEWBERY, Sir? This may come
from another Hand. This is not the
Book, Sir, mentioned in the Title,
but the Introduction to that Book;
and it is intended, Sir, not for those
Sort of Children, but for Children of
six Feet high, of which, as my Friend
has justly observed, there are many
Millions in the Kingdom; and these
Reflections,

Reflections, Sir, have been rendered
neceſſary, by the unaccountable and
diabolical Scheme which many Gentlemen now give into, of laying a
Number of Farms into one, and very
often of a whole Pariſh into one
Farm; which in the End muſt reduce
the common People to a State of Vaſ-
ſalage, worſe than that under the Ba-
rons of old, or of the Clans in *Scot-*
land; and will in Time depopulate
the Kingdom. But as you are tired
of the Subject, I ſhall take myſelf
away, and you may viſit *Little Mar-*
gery. So, Sir, your Servant,

The EDITOR.

C H A P.

CHAP. I.

How and about Little Margery *and her* Brother.

CARE and Diſcontent ſhortened the Days of Little *Margery's* Father.---He was forced from his Family, and ſeized with a violent Fever in a Place where Dr. *James's* Powder was not to be had, and where he died miſerably. *Margery's* poor Mother ſurvived the Loſs of her Huſband but a few Days, and died of a broken Heart, leaving *Margery* and her little Brother to the wide World ; but, poor Woman, it would have melted your Heart to have ſeen how frequently ſhe heaved up her Head, while ſhe lay ſpeechleſs, to ſurvey with languiſhing Looks her little Orphans,

as much as to say, *Do Tommy, do
Margery come with me.* They cried
poor Things, and she sighed away
her Soul; and I hope is happy.

It would both have excited your Pity,
and have done your Heart good, to
have seen how fond these two little
ones were of each other, and how,
Hand in Hand, they trotted about.
Pray see them.

They

They were both very ragged, and
Tommy had two Shoes, but *Margery*
had but one.   They had nothing,
poor Things, to fupport them (not
being in their own Parifh) but what
they picked from the Hedges, or got
from the poor People, and they lay
every Night in a Barn.   Their Relations took no Notice of them ; no,
they were rich and afhamed to own
                                    fuch

such a poor little ragged Girl as *Margery*, and such a dirty little curl-pated Boy as *Tommy*. Our Relations and Friends seldom take Notice of us when we are poor; but as we grow rich they grow fond. And this will always be the Case, while People love Money better than Virtue, or better than they do God Almighty. But such wicked Folks, who love nothing but Money, and are proud and despise the Poor, never come to any good in the End, as we shall see by and by.

C H A P. II.

How and about Mr. Smith.

MR. *Smith* was a very worthy Clergyman, who lived in the Parish where Little *Margery* and
Tommy

Tommy were born; and having a Relation come to fee him, who was **a** charitable good Man, he fent for thefe Children to him. The Gentleman ordered Little *Margery* a new Pair of Shoes, gave Mr. *Smith* fome Money to buy her Cloathes; **and** faid, he would take *Tommy* and make him a little Sailor; and accordingly had a Jacket and Trowfers made for him, in which he now appears. Pray look at him.

B   After

After some Days the Gentleman
intended to go to *London*, and take
little *Tommy* with him, of whom you
will know more by and by, for we
shall at a proper Time present you
with some Part of his History, his
Travels and Adventures.

The Parting between these two little Children was very affecting, *Tom-*
my cried and *Margery* cried, and they
kissed each other an hundred Times.
At last *Tommy* thus wiped off her Tears

wit

with the End of his Jacket, and bid her cry no more, for that he would come to her again, when he returned from Sea. However, as they were so very fond, the Gentleman would not suffer them to take Leave of each other; but told *Tommy* he should ride out with him, and come back at Night. When Night came, Little *Margery* grew very uneasy about her Brother, and after sitting up as late as Mr. *Smith* would let her, she went crying to Bed.

C H A P. III.

How Little Margery obtained the Name of Goody Two-Shoes, and what happened in the Parish.

AS soon as Little *Margery* got up in the Morning, which was

very

very early, she ran all round the Village, crying for her Brother and after some Time returned greatly distressed. However, at this Instant, the Shoemaker very opportunely came in with the new Shoes, for which she had been measured by the Gentleman's Order.

Nothing could have supported Little *Margery* under the Affliction she was in for the Loss of her Brother, but the Pleasure she took in her *two* Shoes. She ran out to Mrs. *Smith* as soon as they were put on, and stroking down her ragged Apron thus,

crie

cried out, *Two Shoes, Mame, see two
Shoes*.   And so she behaved to all the
People she met, and by that Means
obtained the Name of *Goody Two
Shoes*, though her Playmates called
her *Old Goody Two Shoes*.

Little *Margery* was very happy in
being with Mr. and Mrs. *Smith*, who
were very charitable and good to her,
and had agreed to breed her up with
B 3   their

their Family; but as soon as that
Tyrant of the Parish, that *Graspall*,
heard of her being there, he applied
first to Mr. *Smith*, and threatened to
reduce his Tythes if he kept her; and
after that he spoke to Sir *Timothy*,
who sent Mr. *Smith* a peremptory
Message by his Servant, that *he should
send back* Meanwell's *Girl to be kept
by her Relations, and not harbour her
in the Parish.* This so distressed Mr.
Smith that he shed Tears, and cried,
Lord have Mercy on the Poor!

The Prayers of the Righteous fly
upwards, and reach unto the Throne
of Heaven, as will be seen in the
Sequel.

Mrs. *Smith* was also greatly concerned at being thus obliged to dis-
card poor Little *Margery.* She kissed
her and cried ;

as

as also did Mr. *Smith*, but they were
obliged to send her away; for the
People who had ruined her Father
could at any Time have ruined
them.

B 4   CHAP.

C H A P. IV.

How Little Margery *learned to read, and by Degrees taught others.*

LITTLE *Margery* saw how good, and how wise Mr. *Smith* was, and concluded, that this was owing to his great Learning, therefore she wanted of all Things to learn to read. For this Purpose she used to meet the little Boys and Girls as they came from School, borrow their Books, and sit down and read till they returned;

By this Means she soon got more Learning than any of her Playmates, and
laid the following Scheme for instructing those who were more ignorant than herself. She found, that
only the following Letters were re-
quired to spell all the Words in the
World; but as some of these Letters
are large and some small, she with
her

her Knife cut out of several Pieces
of Wood ten Setts of each of these:

a b c d e f g h i j k l m n o
p q r ſ s t u v w x y z.

And ſix Setts of theſe:

A B C D E F G H I K L M N
O P Q R S T U V W X Y Z.

And having got an old Spelling-
Book, ſhe made her Companions ſet
up all the Words they wanted to ſpell,
and after that ſhe taught them to
compoſe Sentences.   You know what
a Sentence is, my Dear, *I will be
good,* is a Sentence; and is made up,
as you ſee, of ſeveral Words.

   The uſual Manner of Spelling, or
carrying on the Game, as they called
                                    it,

it, was this: Suppofe the Word to
be fpelt was Plumb Pudding (and
who can fuppofe a better) the Children were placed in a Circle, and
the firft brought the Letter *P*, the
next *l*, the next *u*, the next *m*, and
fo on till the whole was fpelt; and
if any one brought a wrong Letter,
he was to pay a Fine, or play no
more. This was at their Play; and
every Morning fhe ufed to go round
to teach the Children with thefe
Rattle-traps in a Bafket, as you fee
in the Print.

once

I once went her Rounds with her,
and was highly diverted, as you may
be, if you please to look into the
next Chapter.

CHAP. V.

How Little Two-Shoes *became a trot-*
ting Tutoress, and how she taught
her young Pupils.

IT was about Seven o'Clock in the
Morning when we set out on this
important

important Bufinefs, and the firft
Houfe we came to was Farmer *Wilfon's*.   See here it is.

Here *Margery* ftopped, and ran up
to the Door. *Tap, tap, tap*. Who's
there? Only little goody *Two Shoes*,
anfwered *Margery*, come to teach
Billy. Oh Little *Goody*, fays Mrs.
Wilfon, with Pleafure in her Face,
I am glad to fee you, *Billy* wants
                                    you

you sadly, for he has learned all his
Lesson. Then out came the little
Boy. *How do doody, Two Shoes*, says
he, not able to speak plain. Yet this
little Boy had learned all his Letters;
for she threw down this Alphabet
mixed together thus:

b d f h k m o q s u w y z ſ
a c e g i l n p r t v x j.

and he picked them up, called them
by their right Names, and put them
all in order thus:

a b c d e f g h i j k l m n o
p q r ſ s t u v w x y z.

She then threw down the Alphabet
of Capital Letters in the Manner you
here see them.

B D

B D F H K M O Q S U W Y Z
A C E G I L N P R T V X J.

an'd he picked them all up, and having told their Names, placed them thus:

A B C D E F G H I J K L M
N O P Q R S T U V W X Y Z.

Now, pray little Reader, take this Bodkin, and see if you can point out the Letters from these mixed Alphabets, and tell how they should be placed as well as little Boy *Billy*.

The next Place we came to was Farmer *Simpson*'s, and here it is.

Bow wow wow, says the Dog at
the Door. Sirrah, says his Mistress,
what do you bark at Little *Two-
Shoes.* Come in *Madge*; here, *Sally*
wants you sadly, she has learned all
her Lesson. Then out came the little one: So *Madge!* says she; so *Sally!* answered the other, have you
learned your Lesson? Yes, that's
what I have, replied the little one in
the

the Country Manner; and immediately taking the Letters she set up these Syllables.

ba be bi bo bu ca ce ci co cu
da de di do du fa fe fi fo fu.

and gave them their exact Sounds as she composed them; after which she set up the following:

ac ec ic oc uc, ad ed id od ud
af ef if of uf, ag eg ig og ug

And pronounced them likewise. She then sung the Cuzz's Chorus (which may be found in the *Little Pretty Play Thing* published by Mr. NEWBERY) and to the same Tune to which it is there set.

After this Little *Two Shoes* taught her to spell Words of one syllable,

C

and

and ſhe ſoon ſet up Pear, Plumb,
Top, Ball, Pin, Puſs, Dog, Hog,
Fawn, Buck, Doe, Lamb, Sheep,
Ram, Cow, Bull, Cock, Hen, and
many more.

The next Place we came to was
Gaffer Cook's Cottage; there you ſee
it before you.

Here a Number of poor Children
where met to learn; who all came
round

round Little *Margery* at once; and, having pulled out her Letters, she asked the little Boy next her, what he had for Dinner? Who answered, *Bread.* (the poor Children in many Places live very hard) Well then, says she, set the first Letter. He put up the Letter B, to which the next added r, and the next e, the next a, the next d, and it stood thus, *Bread.*

And what had you *Polly Comb* for your Dinner? *Apple-pye,* answered the little Girl: Upon which the next in Turn set up a great A, the next a p each, and so on till the two Words Apple and Pye were united and stood thus, *Apple-pye.*

The next had *Potatoes,* the next *Beef and Turnips,* which were spelt with many others, till the Game

C 2   of

of Spelling was finished. She then set them another Task, and we proceeded.

The next Place we came to was Farmer *Thompson's*, where there were a great many little ones waiting for her.

So little Mrs. *Goody Two-Shoes*, says one of them, where have you been so long? I have been teaching, says she, longer than I intended, and am afraid I am come too soon for you now. No, but indeed you are not, replied the other; for I have got my Lesson, and so has *Sally Dawson*, and so has *Harry Wilson*, and so we have all; and they capered about as if they were overjoyed to see her. Why then, says she, you are all very good, and GOD Almighty will love you; so let us begin our Lessons. They all huddled round her,

her, and though at the other Place
they were employed about Words and
Syllables, here we had People of
much greater Underſtanding who
dealt only in Sentences.

The Letters being brought upon
the Table, one of the little ones ſet
up the following Sentence.

*The Lord have Mercy upon me, and
grant that I may be always good, and
ſay my Prayers, and love the Lord my
God with all my Heart, with all my
Soul, and with all my Strength ; and
honour the King, and all good Men in
Authority under him.*

Then the next took the Letters,
and compoſed this Sentence.

*Lord have Mercy upon me, and grant
that I may love my Neighbour as myſelf,
and do unto all Men as I would have
them do unto me, and tell no Lies ; but be
honeſt and juſt in all my Dealings.*

The third composed the following Sentence.

The Lord have Mercy upon me, and grant that I may honour my Father and Mother, and love my Brothers and Sisters, Relations and Friends, and all my Playmates, and every Body, and endeavour to make them happy.

The fourth composed the following.

I pray God *to bless this whole Company, and all our Friends, and all our Enemies.*

To this last *Polly Sullen* objected, and said, truly, she did not know why she should pray for her Enemies? Not pray for your Enemies, says Little *Margery* ; yes, you must, you are no Christian, if you don't forgive your Enemies, and do Good for Evil. *Polly* still pouted, upon which Little *Margery* said, though she was

poor,

poor, and obliged to lie in a Barn,
she would not keep Company with
such a naughty, proud, perverse Girl
as *Polly* ; and was going away ; however the Difference was made up, and
she set them to compose the following

LESSONS
For the CONDUCT of LIFE,

LESSON I.

He that will thrive,
Must rise by Five.
He that hath thriv'n
May lie till Seven.
Truth may be blam'd,
But cannot be sham'd.
Tell me with whom you go ;
And I'll tell what you do.

C 4

A Friend in your Need,
Is a Friend indeed.
They ne'er can be wife,
Who good Counfel defpife.

Lesson II.

A wife Head makes a clofe Mouth.

Don't burn your Lips with another Man's Broth.

Wit is Folly, unlefs a wife Man hath the Keeping of it.

Ufe foft Words and hard Arguments.

Honey catches more Flies than Vinegar.

To forget a Wrong is the beft Revenge.

Patience is a Plaifter for all Sores.

Where Pride goes, Shame will follow.

When Vice enters the Room, Vengeance is near the Door.

Induftry

Industry is Fortune's right Hand, and
    Frugality her left.

Make much of Three-pence, or you
    ne'er will be worth a Groat.

LESSON III.

A Lie stands upon one Leg, but
    Truth upon two.

When a Man talks much, believe
    but half what he says.

Fair Words butter no Parsnips.

Bad Company poisons the Mind.

A covetous Man is never satisfied.

Abundance, like Want, ruins many.

Contentment is the best Fortune.

A contented Mind is a continual Feast.

A LESSON in Religion.

Love GOD, for he is good.

Fear GOD, for he is just.

Pray

Pray to GOD, for all good Things
    come from him.

Praise GOD, for great is his Mercy
    towards us, and wonderful are
    all his Works.

Those who strive to be good, have
    GOD on their Side.

Those who have GOD for their
    Friend, shall want nothing.

Confess your Sins to GOD, and if
    you repent he will forgive you.

Remember that all you do, is done in
    the Presence of GOD.

The Time will come, my Friends,
    when we must give

Account to GOD, how we on Earth
    did live.

A Moral LESSON.

A good Boy will make a good Man.

Honour your Parents, and the World
    will honour you.

Love

Love your Friends, and your Friends
will love you.

He that ſwims in Sin, will ſink in
Sorrow.

Learn to live, as you would wiſh to
die.

As you expect all Men ſhould deal
by you :

So deal by them, and give each
Man his Due.

As we were returning home, we
ſaw a Gentleman, who was very ill,
ſitting under a ſhady Tree at the
Corner of his Rookery. Though ill,
he began to joke with Little *Margery*, and ſaid, laughingly, ſo, *Goody
Two-Shoes*, they tell me you are a
cunning little Baggage ; pray, can
you tell me what I ſhall do to get
well ?   Yes, Sir, ſays ſhe, go to
Bed

Bed when your Rooks do. You see
they are going to Rest already:

Do you so likewise, and get up with
them in the Morning ; earn, as they
do, every Day what you eat, and eat
and drink no more than you earn ;
and you'll get Health and keep it.
What should induce the Rooks to
frequent Gentlemens Houses only,
but to tell them how to lead a prudent

dent Life? They never build over Cottages or Farm-houses, because they see, that these People know how to live without their Admonition.

Thus Health and Wit you may improve,
Taught by the Tenants of the Grove.

The Gentleman laughing gave *Margery* Six-pence, and told her she was a sensible Hussey.

C H A P. VI.

How the whole Parish was frighted.

WHO does not know Lady *Ducklington*, or who does not know that she was buried at this Parish Church?

Well,

Well, I never saw so grand a Funeral in all my Life; but the Money they squandered away, would have been better laid out in little Books for Children, or in Meat, Drink, and Cloaths for the Poor.

This is a fine Hearse indeed, and the nodding Plumes on the Horses

look

look very grand ; but what End does that anſwer, otherwiſe than to diſplay the Pride of the Living, or the Vanity of the Dead. Fie upon ſuch Folly, ſay I, and Heaven grant that thoſe who want more Senſe may have it.

But all the Country round came to ſee the Burying, and it was late before the Corpſe was interred. Af-

ter

ter which, in the Night, or rather
about Four o'Clock in the Morning,
the Bells were heard to jingle in the
Steeple, which frightened the People
prodigiously, who all thought it was
Lady *Ducklington*'s Ghost dancing a-
mong the Bell-ropes. The People
flocked to *Will Dobbins* the Clerk,
and wanted him to go and see what
it was, but *William* said, he was sure
it was a Ghost, and that he would
not offer to open the Door. At length
Mr. *Long* the Rector, hearing such
an Uproar in the Village, went to
the Clerk, to know why he did not
go into the Church, and see who was
there. I go, Sir, says *William*, why
the Ghost would frighten me out of
my Wits.--- Mrs. *Dobbins* too cried,
and laying hold of her Husband said,
he should not be eat up by the Ghost.
A Ghost, you Blockheads, says Mr.

Long in a Pet, did either of you ever see a Ghost, or know any Body that did? Yes, says the Clerk, my Father did once in the Shape of a Windmill, and it walked all round the Church in a white Sheet, with Jack Boots on, and had a Gun by its Side instead of a Sword. A fine Picture of a Ghost truly, says Mr. *Long*, give me the Key of the Church, you Monkey; for I tell you there is no such Thing now, whatever may have been formerly.——Then taking the Key, he went to the Church, all the People following him. As soon as he had opened the Door, what Sort of a Ghost do ye think appeared? Why Little *Two Shoes*, who being weary had fallen asleep in one of the Pews during the Funeral Service, and was shut in all Night. She immediately asked Mr. *Long*'s Pardon for the

D   Trouble

Trouble she had given him, told
him, she had been locked into the
Church, and said, she should not
have rung the Bells, but that she was
very cold, and hearing Farmer *Boult's*
Man go whistling by with his Horses,
she was in Hopes he would have went
to the Clerk for the Key to let her
out.

C H A P.

CHAP. VII.

Containing an Account of all the Spi-
rits, or Ghosts, she saw in the
Church.

THE People were ashamed to ask
Little *Madge* any Questions before Mr. *Long*, but as soon as he was
gone, they all got round her to sa-
tisfy their Curiosity, and desired she
would give them a particular Account of all that she had heard and
seen.

Her T A L E.

I went to the Church, said she, as
most of you did last Night, to see the
Burying, and being very weary, I
sate me down in Mr. *Jones's* Pew.

and

and fell fast asleep. At Eleven of the
Clock I awoke; which I believe was
in some measure occasioned by the
Clock's striking, for I heard it. I
started up, and could not at first tell
where I was; but after some Time
I recollected the Funeral, and soon
found that I was shut in the Church.
It was dismal dark, and I could see
nothing; but while I was standing in
the Pew, something jumped up upon
me behind, and laid, as I thought,
its Hands over my Shoulders.---- I
own, I was a little afraid at first;
however, I considered that I had always been constant at Prayers and at
Church, and that I had done nobody
any Harm, but had endeavoured to
do what Good I could; and then,
thought I, what have I to fear? yet
I kneeled down to say my Prayers.
As soon as I was on my Knees something

thing very cold, as cold as Marble,
ay, as cold as Ice, touched my Neck,
which made me ſtart; however, I
continued my Prayers, and having
begged Protection from Almighty
GOD, I found my Spirits come, and I
was ſenſible that I had nothing to fear;
for GOD Almighty protects not only
all thoſe who are good, but alſo all
thoſe who endeavour to be good. ----
Nothing can withſtand the Power,
and exceed the Goodneſs of GOD Almighty. Armed with the Confidence
of his Protection, I walked down the
Church Iſle, when I heard ſomething,
pit pat, pit pat, pit pat, come after
me, and ſomething touched my Hand,
which ſeemed as cold as a Marble
Monument. I could not think what
this was, yet I knew it could not
hurt me, and therefore I made myſelf eaſy, but being very cold, and

the

the Church being paved with Stone,
which was very damp, I felt my Way
as well as I could to the Pulpit, in
doing which something brushed by
me, and almost threw me down.
However I was not frightened, for
I knew, that God Almighty would
suffer nothing to hurt me.

At last, I found out the Pulpit,
and having shut too the Door, I laid
me down on the Mat and Cushion
to sleep; when something thrust and
pulled the Door, as I thought for
Admittance, which prevented my going to sleep. At last it cries, *Bow*,
wow, *wow*; and I concluded it
must be Mr. *Saunderson*'s Dog, which
had followed me from their House to
Church, so I opened the Door, and
called *Snip*, *Snip*, and the Dog jumped up upon me immediately. After
this *Snip* and I lay down together,
and

and had a most comfortable Nap; for when I awoke again it was almost light, I then walked up and down all the Isles of the Church to keep myself warm; and though I went into the Vault, and trod on Lady *Ducklington*'s Coffin, I saw no Ghost, and I believe it was owing to the Reason Mr. *Long* has given you, namely, that there is no such Thing to be seen. As to my Part, I would as soon lie all Night in the Church as in any other Place; and I am sure that any little Boy or Girl, who is good, and loves God Almighty, and keeps his Commandments, may as safely lie in the Church, or the Church-yard, as any where else, if they take Care not to get Cold; for I am sure there are no Ghosts, either to hurt, or to frighten them; though any one possessed of Fear

D 4   might

might have taken Neighbour *Saun-derson's* Dog with his cold Nose for a Ghost; and if they had not been un-deceived, as I was, would never have thought otherwise. All the Company acknowledged the Justness of the Observation, and thanked Little *Two Shoes* for her Advice.

REFLECTION.

After this, my dear Children, I hope you will not believe any foolish Stories that ignorant, weak, or de-signing People may tell you about *Ghosts*; for the Tales of *Ghosts*, *Witches*, and *Fairies*, are the Frolicks of a distempered Brain. No wise Man ever saw either of them. Little *Margery* you see was not afraid; no, she had *good Sense*, and a *good Conscience*, which is a Cure for all these imaginary Evils.

CHAP.

C H A P. VIII.

Of something which happened to Little Two-Shoes in a Barn, more dreadful than the Ghost in the Church; and how she returned Good for Evil to her Enemy Sir Timothy.

SOME Days after this a more dreadful Accident befel Little *Madge.* She happened to be coming late from teaching, when it rained, thundered, and lightened, and therefore she took Shelter in a Farmer's Barn

at a Diftance from the Village. Soon after, the Tempeft drove in four Thieves,
who, not feeing fuch a little creep-
moufe Girl as *Two Shoes*, lay down
on the Bay next to her, and began to
talk over their Exploits, and to fettle
Plans for future Robberies. Little
Margery on hearing them, covered
herfelf with Straw. To be fure fhe
was fadly frighted, but her good
Senfe

Senfe taught her, that the only Security fhe had was in keeping herfelf
concealed; therefore fhe laid very
ftill, and breathed very foftly. About
Four o'Clock thefe wicked People
came to a Refolution to break both
Sir *William Dove*'s Houfe, and Sir
Timothy Gripe's. and by Force of Arms
to carry off all their Money, Plate
and Jewels; but as it was thought
then too late, they agreed to defer it
till the next Night. After laying this
Scheme they all fet out upon their
Pranks, which greatly rejoiced *Margery*, as it would any other little Girl
in her Situation. Early in the Morning fhe went to Sir *William*, and told
him the whole of their Converfation.
Upon which, he afked her Name,
gave her Something, and bid her call
at his Houfe the Day following. She
alfo went to Sir *Timothy*, notwith-
　　　　　　　　　ftanding

standing he had used her so ill; for
she knew it was her Duty to *do Good
for Evil*.   As soon as he was informed who she was, he took no Notice
of her; upon which she desired to
speak to Lady *Gripe*; and having informed her Ladyship of the Affair,
she went her Way.   This Lady had
more Sense than her Husband, which
indeed is not a singular Case; for instead of despising Little *Margery* and
her Information, she privately set
People to guard the House.   The
Robbers divided themselves, and
went about the Time mentioned to
both Houses, and were surprized by
the Guards, and taken.   Upon exa-
mining these Wretches, one of which
turned Evidence, both Sir *William*
and Sir *Timothy* found that they ow-
ed their Lives to the Discovery made
by Little *Margery*; and the first took
                                    great

great Notice of her, and would no longer let her lie in a Barn; but Sir *Timothy* only said, that he was ashamed to owe his Life to the Daughter of one who was his Enemy; so true it is, *that a proud Man seldom forgives those he has injured.*

CHAP. IX.

How Little Margery *was made Principal of a Country College.*

MRS. *Williams*, of whom I have given a particular Account in my *New Year's Gift*, and who kept a College for instructing little Gentlemen and Ladies in the Science of A, B, C, was at this Time very old and infirm, and wanted to decline that important Trust. This being told to Sir *William Dove*, who lived

in

in the Parish, he sent for Mrs. *Wil-*
liams, and desired she would examine
Little *Two Shoes*, and see whether
she was qualified for the Office.----
This was done, and Mrs. *Williams*
made the following Report in her
Favour, namely, *that Little* Margery
was the best Scholar, and had the best
Head, and the best Heart of any one
she had examined. All the Country
had a great Opinion of Mrs. *Willi-*
ams, and this Character gave them
also a great Opinion of Mrs. *Marge-*
ry ; for so we must now call her.

This Mrs. *Margery* thought the
happiest Period of her Life ; but
more Happiness was in Store for her.
God Almighty heaps up Blessings for
all those who love him, and though
for a Time he may suffer them to be
poor and distressed, and hide his good
Purposes from human Sight, yet in
the

the End they are generally crowned with Happiness here, and no one can doubt of their being so hereafter.

On this Occasion the following Hymn, or rather a Translation of the twenty-third Psalm, is said to have been written, and was soon after published in the *Spectator*.

I.

The Lord my Pasture shall prepare,
And feed me with a Shepherd's Care:
His Presence shall my Wants supply,
And guard me with a watchful Eye;
My Noon-day Walks he shall attend,
And all my Midnight Hours defend.

II.

When in the sultry Glebe I faint,
Or on the thirsty Mountain pant;
To fertile Vales and dewy Meads,
My weary wand'ring Steps he leads;
Where peaceful Rivers, soft and slow,
Amid the verdant Landskip flow.

III. Tho'

III.

Tho' in the Paths of Death I tread,
With gloomy Horrors overspread,
My stedfast Heart shall fear no Ill,
For thou, O Lord, art with me still;
Thy friendly Crook shall give me Aid,
And guide me thro'the dreadful Shade.

IV.

Tho' in a bare and rugged Way,
Thro' devious lonely Wilds I stray,
Thy Bounty shall my Pains beguile :
The barren Wilderness shall smile,
With sudden Greens & herbage crown'd
And Streams shall murmur all around.

Here ends the History of Little *Two Shoes.* Those who would know how she behaved after she came to be Mrs. *Margery Two Shoes* must read the Second Part of this Work, in which an Account of the Remainder of her Life, her Marriage, and Death are set forth at large, according to Act of Parliament.   The

The Renowned
HISTORY
OF
Mrs. Margery Two-Shoes.

Introduction.

IN the First Part of this Work, the young Student has read, and I hope with Pleasure and Improvement, the History of this Lady, while she was known and distinguished by the Name of *Little Two Shoes*; we are now come to a Period of her Life when that Name was discarded, and a more eminent one bestowed upon her, I mean, that of Mrs. *Margery Two Shoes*: For as she was now President

of

of the A, B, C College, it became necessary to exalt her in Title as well as in Place.

No sooner was she settled in this Office, but she laid every possible Scheme to promote the Welfare and Happiness of all her Neighbours, and especially of the Little Ones, in whom she took great Delight, and all those whose Parents could not afford to pay for their Education, she taught for nothing, but the Pleasure she had in their Company, for you are to observe, that they were very good, or were soon made so by her good Management.

CHAP.

CHAP. I.

Of her School, her Ushers, or Assistants, and her Manner of Teaching.

WE have already informed the Reader, that the School where she taught, was that which was before kept by Mrs. *Williams*, whose Character you may find in my *New Year's Gift*. The Room was large, and as she knew, that Nature intended Children should be always in Action, she placed her different Letters, or Alphabets, all round the School, so that every one was obliged to get up to fetch a Letter, or to spell a Word, when it came to their Turn; which not only kept them in Health, but fixed the Letters and Points firmly in their Minds.

E 2   She

She had the following Assistants or Ushers to help her, and I will tell you how she came by them. Mrs. *Margery*, you must know, was very humane and compassionate; and her Tenderness extended not only to all Mankind, but even to all Animals that were not noxious; as your's ought to do, if you would be happy here, and go to Heaven hereafter. These are God Almighty's Creatures as well as we. He made both them and us; and for wise Purposes, best known to himself, placed them in this World to live among us; so that they are our fellow Tenants of the Globe. How then can People dare to torture and wantonly destroy God Almighty's Creatures? They as well as you are capable of feeling Pain, and of receiving Pleasure, and how can you, who want to be made hap-

py

py yourself, delight in making your fellow Creatures miserable? Do you think the poor Birds, whose Nest and young Ones that wicked Boy *Dick Wilson* ran away with Yesterday, do not feel as much Pain, as your Father and Mother would have felt, had any one pulled down their House and ran away with you? To be sure they do. Mrs. *Two Shoes* used to speak of those Things, and of naughty Boys throwing at Cocks, torturing Flies, and whipping Horses and Dogs with Tears in her Eyes, and would never suffer any one to come to her School who did so.

One Day, as she was going through the next Village, she met with some wicked Boys who had got a young Raven, which they were going to throw at, she wanted to get the poor Creature out of their cruel Hands,

and

and therefore gave them a Penny for him, and brought him home. She called his Name *Ralph*, and a fine Bird he is. Do look at him.

Now this Bird she taught to speak, to spell and to read; and as he was particularly fond of playing with the large Letters, the Children used to call this *Ralph*'s Alphabet.

A B

A B C D E F G H I J K L M
N O P Q R S T U V W X Y Z.

He always set at her Elbow, as you
see in the first Picture, and when any
of the Children were wrong she used
to call out, *Put them right Ralph.*

Some Days after she had met with
the Raven, as she was walking in the
Fields, she saw some naughty Boys,
who had taken a Pidgeon and tied a
String to its Leg, in order to let it
fly, and draw it back again when
they pleased; and by this Means they
tortured the poor Animal with the
Hopes of Liberty and repeated Disappointment. This Pidgeon she also bought, and taught him how to
spell and read, though not to talk,
and he performed all those extraordinary Things which are recorded of
E 4   the

the famous Bird, that was some Time
since advertised in the *Haymarket*,
and visited by most of the great People in the Kingdom.   This Pidgeon
was a very pretty Fellow, and she
called him *Tom*.   See here he is.

And as the Raven *Ralph* was fond of
the large Letters, *Tom* the Pidgeon
took Care of the small ones, of which
he composed this Alphabet.

a b

a b c d e f g h i j k l m
n o p q r s t u v w x y z.

The Neighbours knowing that
Mrs. *Two Shoes* was very good, as
to be fure nobody was better, made
her a Prefent of a little Sky-lark,
and a fine Bird he is.

Now

Now as many People, even at that Time had learned to lie in Bed long in the Morning, she thought the Lark might be of Use to her and her Pupils, and tell them when to get up.

For he that is fond of his Bed, and lays 'till Noon, lives but half his Days, the rest being lost in Sleep, which is a Kind of Death.

Some Time after this a poor Lamb had lost its Dam, and the Farmer being about to kill it, she bought it of him, and brought it home with her to play with the Children, and teach them when to go to Bed; for it was a Rule with the wise Men of that Age (and a very good one, let me tell you) to

Rise

*Rise with the Lark, and lie down with
the Lamb.*

This Lamb she called *Will*, and a
pretty Fellow he is; do, look at him.

No sooner was *Tippy* the Lark and
Will the Ba-lamb brought into the
School, but that sensible Rogue
Ralph, the Raven, composed the
                              follow-

following Verse, which every little
good Boy and Girl should get by
Heart.

> *Early to Bed, and early to rise;*
> *Is the Way to be healthy, and weal-*
> *thy, and wise.*

A sly Rogue; but it is true enough;
for those who do not go to Bed early cannot rise early; and those who
do not rise early cannot do much
Business. Pray, let this be told at
the Court, and to People who have
Routs and Rackets.

Soon after this, a Present was made
to Mrs. *Margery* of little Dog *Jumper*, and a pretty Dog he is. Pray,
look at him.

Jumper,

Jumper, Jumper, Jumper! He is always in a good Humour, and playing and jumping about, and therefore he was called *Jumper.* The Place assigned for *Jumper* was that of keeping the Door, so that he may be called the Porter of the College, for he would let nobody go out, or any one come in, without the Leave of his Mistress. See how he sits, a saucy Rogue.

Billy

Billy the Ba-lamb was a chearful Fellow, and all the Children were fond of him, wherefore Mrs. *Two-Shoes* made it a Rule, that those who behaved best should have *Will* home with them at Night to carry their Satchel or Basket at his Back, and bring it in the Morning. See what a fine Fellow he is, and how he trudges along.

CHAP. II.

A Scene of Distress in the School.

IT happened one Day, when Mrs. *Two-Shoes* was diverting the Children after Dinner, as she usually did with some innocent Games, or entertaining and instructive Stories, that a Man arrived with the melancholy News of *Sally Jones*'s Father being
thrown

thrown from his Horſe, and thought
paſt all Recovery; nay, the Meſſenger ſaid, that he was ſeemingly dy-
ing, when he came away. Poor *Sally* was greatly diſtreſſed, as indeed
were all the School, for ſhe dearly
loved her Father, and Mrs. *Two-
Shoes*, and all the Children dearly
loved her. It is generally ſaid, that
we never know the real Value of our
Parents or Friends till we have loſt
them; but poor *Sally* felt this by
Affection, and her Miſtreſs knew it
by Experience. All the School were
in Tears, and the Meſſenger was obliged to return; but before he went
Mrs. *Two-Shoes*, unknown to the
Children, ordered *Tom* Pidgeon to
go home with the Man, and bring
a Letter to inform her how Mr.
Jones did. They ſet out together,
and

and the Pidgeon rode on the Man's
Head, (as you see here) for

the Man was able to carry the Pidgeon, though the Pidgeon was not
able to carry the Man, if he had, they
would have been there much sooner,
for *Tom* Pidgeon was *very good*, and
never staid on an Errand.

Soon after the Man was gone the
Pidgeon

Pidgeon was loft, and the Concern the Children were under for *Mr. Jones* and little *Sally* was in fome Meafure diverted, and Part of their Attention turned after *Tom*, who was a great Favourite, and confequently much bewailed. Mrs. *Margery*, who knew the great Ufe and Neceffity of teaching Children to fubmit chearfully to the Will of Providence, bid them wipe away their Tears, and then kiffing *Sally*, you muft be a good Girl, fays fhe, and depend upon God Almighty for his Bleffing and Protection; for *he is a Father to the Fatherlefs, and defendeth all thofe who put their Truft in him.* She then told them a Story, which I fhall relate in as few Words as poffible.

F

The

The History of Mr. Lovewell, *Father to Lady* Lucy.

Mr. *Lovewell* was born at *Bath,* and apprenticed to a laborious Trade in *London,* which being too hard for him, he parted with his Master by Consent, and hired himself as a common Servant to a Merchant in the City. Here he spent his leisure Hours not as Servants too frequently do, in Drinking and Schemes of Pleasure, but in improving his Mind; and among other Acquirements, he made himself a complete Master of Accompts. His Sobriety, Honesty, and the Regard he paid to his Master's Interest, greatly recommended him in the whole Family, and he had several Offices of Trust committed to his Charge, in which he

acquitted

acquitted himself so well, that the Merchant removed him from the Stable into the Counting-house.

Here he soon made himself Master of the Business, and became so useful to the Merchant, that in regard to his faithful Services, and the Affection he had for him, he married him to his own Niece, a prudent agreeable young Lady; and gave him a Share in the Business. See what Honesty and Industry will do for us. Half the great Men in *London*, I am told, have made themselves by this Means, and who would but be honest and industrious, when it is so much our Interest and our Duty.

After some Years the Merchant died, and left Mr. *Lovewell* possessed of many fine Ships at Sea, and much Money, and he was happy in a Wife, who had brought him a Son and two

Daugh-

Daughters, all dutiful and obedient. The Treasures and good Things, however, of this Life are so uncertain, that a Man can never be happy, unless he lays the Foundation for it in his own Mind. So true is that Copy in our Writing Books, which tells us, that *a contented Mind is a continual Feast.*

After some Years successful Trade, he thought his Circumstances sufficient to insure his own Ships, or, in other Words, to send his Ships and Goods to Sea without being insured by others, as is customary among Merchants ; when unfortunately for him, four of them richly laden were lost at Sea. This he supported with becoming Resolution ; but the next Mail brought him Advice, that nine others were taken by the *French*, with whom we were then at War ; and this,

to-

together with the Failure of three foreign Merchants whom he had trusted, compleated his Ruin. He was then obliged to call his Creditors together, who took his Effects, and being angry with him for the imprudent Step of not insuring his Ships, left him destitute of all Subsistence. Nor did the Flatterers of his Fortune, those who had lived by his Bounty when in his Prosperity, pay the least Regard either to him or his Family. So true is another Copy, that you will find in your Writing Book, which says, *Misfortune tries our Friends.* All these Slights of his pretended Friends, and the ill Usage of his Creditors, both he and his Family bore with Christian Fortitude ; but other Calamities fell upon him, which he felt more sensibly.

In this Distress, one of his Relations,

tions, who lived at *Florence*, offered to take his Son; and another, who lived at *Barbadoes*, sent for one of his Daughters. The Ship which his Son sailed in was cast away, and all the Crew supposed to be lost; and the Ship, in which his Daughter went a Passenger, was taken by Pyrates, and one Post brought the miserable Father an Account of the Loss of his two Children. This was the severest Stroke of all : It made him compleatly wretched, and he knew it must have a dreadful Effect on his Wife and Daughter; he therefore endeavoured to conceal it from them. But the perpetual Anxiety he was in, together with the Loss of his Appetite and want of rest, soon alarmed his Wife. She found something was labouring in his Breast, which was concealed from her; and one
Night

Night being difturbed in a Dream,
with what was ever in his Thoughts,
and calling out upon his dear Children; fhe awoke him, and infifted
upon knowing the Caufe of his In-
quietude. *Nothing, my Dear, nothing,*
fays he, *The Lord gave, and the Lord
hath taken away, bleffed be the Name
of the Lord.* This was fufficient to
alarm the poor Woman; fhe lay till
his Spirits were compofed, and as
fhe thought afleep, then ftealing out
of Bed, got the Keys and opened
his Bureau, where fhe found the fa-
tal Account. In the Height of her
Diftractions, fhe flew to her Daughter's Room, and waking her with
her Shrieks, put the Letters into her
Hands. The young Lady, unable
to fupport this Load of Mifery fell
into a Fit, from which it was thought
fhe never could have been recovered.

How-

However, at laſt ſhe revived; but the Shock was ſo great, that it entirely deprived her of her Speech.

Thus loaded with Miſery, and unable to bear the Slights and Diſdain of thoſe who had formerly profeſſed themſelves Friends, this unhappy Family retired into a Country, where they were unknown, in order to hide themſelves from the World; when, to ſupport their Indepency, the Father laboured as well as he could at Huſbandry, and the Mother and Daughter ſometimes got ſpinning and knitting Work, to help to furniſh the Means of Subſiſtence; which however was ſo precarious and uncertain, that they often, for many Weeks together, lived on nothing but Cabbage and Bread boiled in Water. But God never forſaketh the Righteous, nor ſuffereth thoſe to

perish

perish who put their Trust in him. At this Time a Lady, who was just come to England, sent to take a pleasant Seat ready furnished in that Neighbourhood, and the Person who was employed for the Purpose, was ordered to deliver a Bank Note of an hundred Pounds to Mr. *Lovewell*, another hundred to his Wife, and fifty to the Daughter, desiring them to take Possession of the House, and get it well aired against she came down, which would be in two or three Days at most. This, to People who were almost starving, was a sweet and seasonable Relief, and they were all sollicitous to know their Benefactress, but of that the Messenger himself was too ignorant to inform them. However, she came down sooner than was expected, and with Tears embraced them again and a-gain:

gain: After which ſhe told the Father and Mother ſhe had heard from their Daughter who was her Acquaintance, and that ſhe was well and on her return to England. This was the agreeable Subject of their Converſation till after Dinner, when drinking their Healths, ſhe again with Tears ſaluted them, and falling upon her Knees aſked their Bleſſings,

'Tis impoſſible to expreſs the mutual Joy

Joy which this occasioned. Their
Conversation was made up of the
most endearing Expressions, inter-
mingled with Tears and Caresses.
Their Torrent of Joy, however, was
for a Moment interrupted, by a
Chariot which stopped at the Gate,
and which brought as they thought
a very unseasonable Visitor, and
therefore she sent to be excused
from seeing Company.

But

But this had no Effect, for a Gentleman richly dressed jumped out of the Chariot, and pursuing the Servant into the Parlour saluted them round, who were all astonished at his Behaviour. But when the Tears trickled from his Cheeks, the Daughter, who had been some Years dumb, immediately cried out, *my Brother! my Brother! my Brother!* and from that Instant recovered her Speech. The mutual Joy which this occasioned, is better felt than expressed. Those who have proper Sentiments of Humanity, Gratitude, and filial Piety will rejoice at the Event, and those who have a proper Idea of the Goodness of God, and his gracious Providence, will from this, as well as other Instances of his Goodness and Mercy, glorify his holy Name, and magnify his Wisdom and Power, who is a

Shield

Shield to the Righteous, and defendeth all those who put their Trust in
him.

As you, my dear Children, may be
sollicitous to know how this happy
Event was brought about, I must inform you, that Mr. *Lovewell's* Son
when the Ship foundered, had with
some others got into the long Boat, and
was taken up by a Ship at Sea, and
carried to the East Indies, where in
a little Time he made a large Fortune; and the Pirates who took his
Daughter, attempted to rob her of
her Chastity; but finding her inflexi-
ble and determined to die rather than
submit, some of them behaved to her
in a very cruel manner; but others,
who had more Honour and Genero-
sity, became her Defenders; upon
which a Quarrel arose between them,
and the Captain, who was the worst

of the Gang, being killed, the rest of
the Crew carried the Ship into a
Port of the *Manilla* Islands, belonging
to the *Spaniards*; where, when her
Story was known, she was treated
with great Respect, and courted by
a young Gentleman, who was taken
ill of a Fever, and died before the
Marriage was agreed on, but left her
his whole Fortune.

You see, my dear *Sally*, how won-
derfully these People were preserved,
and made happy after such extreme
Distress; we are therefore never to
despair, even under the greatest Misfortunes, for God Almighty is All-
powerful, and can deliver us at any
Time. Remember *Job*, but I think
you have not read so far, take the
Bible, *Billy Jones*, and read the History of that good and patient Man.
At this Instant something was heard

to flap at the Window, *Wow, wow, wow,* fays Jumper, and attempted to leap up and open the Door, at which the Children were furprized; but Mrs. *Margery* knowing what it was, opened the Cafement, as *Noah* did the Window of the Ark, and drew in *Tom* Pidgeon with a Letter, and fee here he is.

As foon as he was placed. **on the** Table, he walked up to little *Sally,* and

and dropping the Letter, cried, *Co,
Co, Coo*, as much as to say, *there read
it*. Now this poor Pidgeon had travelled fifty Miles in about an Hour
to bring *Sally* this Letter, and who
would destroy such pretty Creatures.
———But let us read the Letter.

My dear Sally,

God Almighty has been very merciful, and restored your Pappa to
again, who is now so well as to be
able to sit up. I hear you are a good
Girl, my Dear, and I hope you will
never forget to praise the Lord for
this his great Goodness and Mercy
to us——What a sad Thing it would
have been if your Father had died,
and left both you and me, and little
Tommy in Distress, and without a
Friend : Your Father sends his Blessing

fing with mine----Be good, my dear Child, and God Almighty will alfo blefs you, whofe Blefling is above all Things.

I am, my Dear Sally,

Your ever affectionate Mother,

MARTHA JONES.

C H A P. III.

Of the amazing Sagacity and Inftinct of a little Dog.

SOON after this, a dreadful Accident happened in the School. It was on a *Thurfday* Morning, I very well remember, when the Children having learned their Leffons very foon, fhe had given them Leave to

G   play,

play, and they were all running about the School and diverting themselves with the Birds and the Lamb; at this Time the Dog, all of a sudden, laid hold of his Mistress's Apron, and endeavoured to pull her out of the School. She was at first surprized, however, she followed him to see what he intended. No sooner had he led her into the Garden, but he ran back and pulled out one of the Children in the same manner; upon which she ordered them all to leave the School immediately, and they had not been out five Minutes, before the Top of the House fell in. What a miraculous Deliverance was here! How gracious! How good was God Almighty, to save all these Children from Destruction, and to make Use of such an Instrument, as a little sagacious Animal to accomplish

his

his Divine Will. I should have observed, that as soon as they were all out in the Garden, the Dog came leaping round them to express his Joy, and when the House was fallen, laid himself down quietly by his Mistress.

Some of the Neighbours, who saw the School fall, and who were in great Pain for *Margery* and the little ones, soon spread the News through the Village, and all the Parents terrified for their Children, came crowding in Abundance; they had, however, the Satisfaction to find them all safe, and upon their Knees, with their Mistress, giving God thanks for their happy Deliverance.

ADVICE *from the* MAN *in the* MOON.

Jumper, Jumper, Jumper, what a
pretty

pretty Dog he is, and how senfible?
Had Mankind half the Sagacity of
Jumper, they would guard againft Accidents of this Sort, by having a
public Survey, occafionally made of
all the Houfes in every Parifh (efpe-
cially of thofe, which are old and de-
cayed) and not fuffer them to remain in a crazy State, 'till they fall
down on the Heads of the poor Inha-
bitants, and crufh them to Death.
Why, it was but Yefterday, that a
whole Houfe fell down in *Grace-
church-ftreet*, and another in *Queen's-
ftreet*, and an hundred more are to
tumble, before this Time twelve
Months; fo Friends, take Care of
yourfelves, and tell the Legiflature,
they ought to take Care for you. How
can you be fo carelefs? Moft of your
Evils arife from Carelefnefs and Extravagance, and yet you excufe yourfelves,

felves, and lay the Fault upon Fortune. Fortune is a Fool, and you
are a Blockhead, if you put it in her
Power to play Tricks with you,

> *Yours,*
>
> *The* MAN *in the* MOON.

You are not to wonder, my dear
Reader, that this little Dog fhould
have more Senfe than you, or your
Father, or your Grandfather.

Though God Almighty has made
Man the Lord of the Creation, and
endowed him with Reafon, yet in
many Refpects, he has been altogether as bountiful to other Creatures
of his forming. Some of the Senfes
of other Animals are more acute
than ours, as we find by daily Experience. You know this little Bird,

G 3 *fweet*

sweet Jug, Jug, Jug, 'tis a Nightingale. This little Creature, after she has entertained us with her Songs all the Spring, and bred up her little ones, flies into a foreign Country, and finds her Way over the Great Sea, without any of the Instruments and Helps which Men are obliged to make Use of for that Purpose. Was you as wife as the Nightingale, you

you might make all the Sailors happy, and have twenty thousand Pounds for teaching them the Longitude.

You would not think *Ralph* the Raven half so wise and so good as he is, though you see him here reading his Book. Yet when the Prophet *Elijah*, was obliged to fly from *Ahab* King of *Israel*, and hide himself in a Cave, these Ravens, at the Command of God Almighty, fed him every Day, and preserved his Life.

And the Word of the Lord came unto Elijah, *saying,* Hide thyself by the Brook Cherith, *that is before* Jordan, *and I have commanded the Ravens to feed thee there. And the Ravens brought him Bread and Flesh in the Morning, and Bread and Flesh in the Evening, and he drank of the Brook,* Kings, B. 1. C. 17.

And the pretty Pidgeon when the

World

World was drowned, and he was confined with *Noah* in the Ark, was sent forth by him to see whether the Waters were abated. *And he sent forth a Dove from him, to see if the Waters were abated from off the Face of the Ground. And the Dove came in to him in the Evening, and lo, in her Mouth was an Olive Leaf plucked off:* So Noah *knew that the Waters were abated from off the Earth.* Gen, viii. 8. 11.

As these, and other Animals, are so sensible and kind to us, we ought to be tender and good to them and not beat them about, and kill them, and take away their young ones, as many wicked Boys do. Does not the Horse and the Ass carry you and your Burthens; don't the Ox plough your Ground, the Cow give you Milk, the Sheep cloath your Back,

the

the Dog watch your House, the Goose find you in Quills to write with, the Hen bring Eggs for your Custards and Puddings, and the Cock call you up in the Morning, when you are lazy, and like to hurt yourselves by laying too long in Bed? If so, how can you be so cruel to them, and abuse God Almighty's good Creatures? Go, naughty Boy, go; be sorry for what you have done, and do so no more, that God Almighty may forgive you. *Amen,* say I, again and again. God will bless you, but not unless you are merciful and good.

'The downfal of the School, was a great Misfortune to Mrs. *Margery;* for she not only lost all her Books, but was destitute of a Place to teach in; but Sir William *Dove,* being informed of this, ordered the House to be built at his own Expence, and

'till

'till that could be done, Farmer *Grove* was so kind, as to let her have his large Hall to teach in.

C H A P. IV.

What happened at Farmer Grove's; *and how she gratified him for the Use of his Room.*

WHILE at Mr. *Grove*'s, which was in the Heart of the Village, she not only taught the Children in the Day Time, but the Farmer's Servants, and all the Neighbours, to read and write in the Evening; and it was a constant Practice before they went away, to make them all go to Prayers and sing Psalms. By this Means, the People grew extremely regular, his Servants were always at Home, instead of being

at

at the Ale-house, and he had more Work done than ever. This gave not only Mr. *Grove,* but all the Neighbours, an high Opinion of her good Sense and prudent Behaviour: And she was so much esteemed, that most of the Differences in the Parish were left to her Decision; and if a Man and Wife quarrelled (which sometimes happened in that Part of the Kingdom) both Parties certainly came to her for Advice. Every Body knows, that *Martha Wilson* was a passionate scolding Jade, and that *John* her Husband, was a surly ill-tempered Fellow. These were one Day brought by the Neighbours for *Margery* to talk to them, when they fairly quarrelled before her, and were going to Blows; but she stepping between them, thus addressed the Husband: *John,* says she, you are a Man, and

ought

ought to have more Sense than to fly
in a Passion, at every Word that is
said amiss by your Wife; and *Martha*, says she, you ought to know
your Duty better, than to say any
Thing to aggravate your Husband's
Resentment. These frequent Quarrels, arise from the Indulgence of
your violent Passions; for I know,
you both love one another, notwithstanding what has passed between
you. Now, pray tell me *John*, and
tell me *Martha*, when you have had
a Quarrel the over Night, are you
not both sorry for it the next Day?
They both declared that they were:
Why then, says she, I'll tell you how
to prevent this for the future, if you
will both promise to take my Advice.
They both promised her. You know,
says she, that a small Spark will set
Fire to Tinder, and that Tinder
properly

properly placed will fire a House; an angry Word is with you as that Spark, for you are both as touchy as Tinder, and very often make your own House too hot to hold you. To prevent this, therefore, and to live happily for the future, you must solemnly agree, that if one speaks an angry Word, the other will not answer, 'till he or she has distinctly called over all the Letters in the Alphabet, and the other not reply 'till he has told twenty; by this Means your Passions will be stifled, and Reason will have Time to take the Rule.

This is the best Recipe that was ever given for a married Couple to live in Peace: Though *John* and his Wife frequently attempted to quarr l afterwards, they never could get their Passions to any considerable Height, for there was something so droll in thus carrying on the Dispute, that before they got to the End of the Argument, they saw the Absurdity of it, laughed, kissed, and were Friends.

Just as Mrs. *Margery* had settled this Difference between *John* and his Wife, the Children (who had been sent out to play, while that Business was transacting) returned some in Tears, and others very disconsolate, for the Loss of a little Dormouse they were very fond of, and which was just dead. Mrs. *Margery*, who had the Art of moralizing and drawing Instructions from every Accident, took this Opportunity of reading them a Lecture on the Uncertainty of Life, and the Necessity of being always prepared for Death. You should get up in the Morning, says she, and so conduct yourselves, as if that Day

was

was to be your laſt, and lie down at Night, as if you never expected to ſee this World any more. This may be done, ſays ſhe, without abating of your Chearfulneſs, for you are not to conſider Death as an Evil, but as a Convenience, as an uſeful Pilot, who is to convey you to a Place of greater Happineſs: Therefore, play my dear Children, and be merry, but be innocent and good. The good Man ſets Death at Defiance, for his Darts are only dreadful to the Wicked.

After this, ſhe permitted the Children to bury the little Dormouſe, and deſired one of them to write his Epitaph, and here it is.

Epitaph

Epitaph on a DORMOUSE, *really written by a little* BOY.

I.

In Paper Case,
Hard by this Place,
Dead a poor Dormouse lies;
And soon or late,
Summon'd by Fate,
Each Prince, each Monarch dies.

II.

Ye Sons of Verse,
While I rehearse,
Attend instructive Rhyme,
No Sins had *Dor*,
To answer for;
Repent of yours in Time.

C H A P.

CHAP. V.

The whole History of the Considering Cap, set forth at large for the Benefit of all whom it may concern.

THE great Reputation Mrs. *Margery* acquired by compoſing Differences in Families, and eſpecially, between Man and Wife, induced her to cultivate that Part of her Syſtem of Morality and Œconomy, in order to render it more extenſively uſeful. For this Purpoſe, ſhe contrived what ſhe called a Charm for the Paſſions, which was a conſidering Cap, almoſt as large as a Grenadiers, but of three equal Sides; on the firſt of which was written, I MAY BE WRONG; on the ſecond, IT IS FIFTY TO ONE BUT YOU ARE;

and

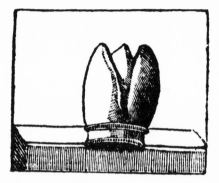

and on the third, I'LL CONSIDER OF
IT.   The other Parts on the out Side,
were filled with odd Characters, as
unintelligible as the Writings of the
old *Egyptians*; But within Side there
was a Direction for its Uſe, of the
utmoſt Conſequence; for it ſtrictly
enjoined to the Poſſeſſor to put on the
Cap, whenever he found his Paſſions
begin to grow turbulent, and not to
delive

deliver a Word whilft it was on, but
with great Coolnefs and Moderation.
As this Cap was an univerfal Cure for
Wrong-headednefs, and prevented
numberlefs Difputes and Quarrels, it
greatly hurt the Trade of the poor
Lawyers, but was of the utmoft Service to the reft of the Community.
They were bought by Hufbands and
Wives, who had themfelves frequent
Occafion for them, and fometimes
lent them to their Children: They
were alfo purchafed in large Quanti-
ties by Mafters and Servants; by
young Folks, who were intent on
Matrimony, by Judges, Jurymen,
and even Phyficians and Divines;
nay, if we may believe Hiftory, the
Legiflators of the Land did not dif-
dain the Ufe of them; and we are
told, that when any important De-
bate arofe, *Cap was the Word,* and

each

each House looked like a grand Synod of *Egyptian* Priests. Nor was this Cap of less Use to Partners in Trade, for with these, as well as with Husband and Wife, if one was out of Humour, the other threw him the Cap, and he was obliged to put it on, and keep it till all was quiet. I myself saw thirteen Caps worn at a Time in one Family, which could not have subsisted an Hour without them ; and I was particularly pleased at Sir *Humphry Huffum's*, to hear a little Girl, when her Father was out of Humour, ask her Mamma, *if she should reach down the Cap ?* These Caps, indeed, were of such Utility, that People of Sense never went without them ; and it was common in the Country, when a Booby made his Appearance, and talked Nonsense, to say, *he had no Cap in his Pocket.*

Advice

Advice from FRIAR BACON.

What was *Fortunatus's* Wishing
Cap, when compared to this? That
Cap, is said to have conveyed People
instantly from one Place to another;
but, as the change of Place does not
change the Temper and Disposition
of the Mind, little Benefit can be
expected from it; nor indeed is much

H 3   to

to be hoped from his famous Purse:
That Purse, it is said, was never empty;
and such a Purse, may be sometimes
convenient; but as Money will not
purchase Peace, it is not necessary
for a Man to encumber himself with
much of it. Peace and Happiness
depend so much upon the State of a
Man's own Mind, and upon the Use
of the considering Cap, that it is generally his own Fault, if he is miserable. One of these Caps will last
a Man his whole Life, and in a Dif-
covery of much greater Importance
to the Public than the Philosopher's
Stone; remember what was said by
my Brazen Head, *Time is, Time was,
Time is Past :* Now the *Time is,* therefore buy the Cap immediately, and
make a proper Use of it, and be happy before the *Time is past.*

Yours, ROGER BACON.

C H A P.

CHAP. VI.

How Mrs. MARGERY *was taken up for a Witch, and what happened on that Occasion.*

AND so it is true? And they have taken up Mrs. *Margery* then, and accused her of being a Witch, only because she was wiser than some of her Neighbours! Mercy upon me! People stuff Children's Heads with Stories of Ghosts, Faries, Witches, and such Nonsense when they are young, and so they continue Fools all their Days. The whole World ought to be made acquainted with her Case, and here it is at their Service.

The Case of Mrs. MARGERY.

Mrs. *Margery,* as we have frequent-ly observed, was always doing good,

and

and thought she could never sufficiently gratify those who had done any Thing to serve her. These generous Sentiments, naturally led her to consult the Interest of Mr. *Grove*, and the rest of her Neighbours ; and as most of their Lands were Meadow, and they depended much on their Hay, which had been for many Years greatly damaged by wet Weather, she contrived an Instrument to direct them when to mow their Grass with Safety, and prevent their Hay being spoiled. They all came to her for Advice, and by that Means got in their Hay without Damage, while most of that in the neighbouring Villages was spoiled.

This made a great Noise in the Country, and so provoked were the People in the other Parishes, that they accused her of being a Witch, and
                                          sent

ïent *Gaffer Goosecap*, a busy Fellow
in other People's Concerns, to find out
Evidence against her. This Wiseacre happened to come to her School,
when she was walking about with the
Raven on one Shoulder, the Pidgeon
on the other, the Lark on her Hand,
and the Lamb and the Dog by her
Side; which indeed made a Droll
Figure, and so surprized the Man,
that he cried out,

a Witch!

a Witch! a Witch! upon this she laughing, answered, a Conjurer! a Conjurer! and so they parted; but it did not end thus, for a Warrant was issued out against Mrs. *Margery,* and she was carried to a Meeting of the Justices, whither all the Neighbours followed her.

At the Meeting, one of the Justices, who knew little of Life, and less of the Law, behaved very idly; and though no Body was able to prove any Thing against her, asked, who she could bring to her Character? *Who* can you bring a-against my Character, Sir, says she, there are People enough who would appear in my Defence, were it necessary; but I never supposed that any one here could be so weak, as to believe there was any such Thing as a Witch. If I am a Witch, this is my

Charm,

Charm, and (laying a Barometer or Weather Glass on the Table) 'tis with this, says she, that I have taught my Neighbours to know the State of the Weather. All the Company laughed, and Sir *William Dove*, who was on the Bench, asked her Accusers, how they could be such Fools, as to think there was any such Thing as a Witch. It is true, continued he, many innocent and worthy People have been abused and even murdered on this absurd and foolish Supposition; which is a Scandal to our Religion, to our Laws, to our Nation, and to common Sense; but I will tell you a Story.

There was in the West of *England* a poor industrious Woman, who laboured under the same evil Report, which this good Woman is accused of. Every Hog that died with the

Murrain,

Murrain, every Cow that flipt her Calf, she was accountable for: If a Horse had the Staggers, she was supposed to be in his Head; and whenever the Wind blew a little harder than ordinary, *Goody Giles* was playing her Tricks, and riding upon a Broomstick in the Air. These, and a thousand other Phantasies, too ridiculous to recite, possessed the Pates of the common People: Horse-shoes were nailed with the Heels upwards, and many Tricks made use of, to mortify the poor Creature; and such was their Rage against her, that they petitioned Mr. *Williams*, the Parson of the Parish, not to let her come to Church; and, at last, even insisted upon it: But this he over-ruled, and allowed the poor old Woman a Nook in one of the Isles to herself, where she muttered over her Prayers in the

best

beſt Manner ſhe could. The Pariſh, thus diſconcerted and enraged, with-drew the ſmall Pittance they allowed for her Support, and would have re-duced her to the Neceſſity of ſtarv-ing, had ſhe not been ſtill aſſiſted by the benevolent Mr. *Williams.*

But I haſten to the Sequel of my Story, in which you will find, that the true Source from whence Witch-craft ſprings is *Poverty, Age,* and *Ignorance*; and that it is impoſſible for a Woman to paſs for a Witch, unleſs ſhe is *very poor, very old,* and lives in a Neighbourhood where the People are *void of common Senſe.*

Some time after, a Brother of her's died in *London,* who, tho' he would not part with a Farthing while he lived, at his Death was obliged to leave her five thouſand Pounds, that he could not carry with him ---This

―――This altered the Face of *Jane*'s Affairs prodigiouſly: She was no longer *Jane*, alias *Joan Giles*, the ugly old Witch, but Madam *Giles*; her old ragged Garb was exchanged for one that was new and genteel; her greateſt Enemies made their Court to her, even the Juſtice himſelf came to wiſh her Joy; and tho' ſeveral Hogs and Horſes died, and the Wind frequently blew afterwards, yet Madam *Giles* was never ſuppoſed to have a Hand in it; and from hence it is plain, as I obſerved before, that a Woman muſt be *very poor*, *very old*, and live in a Neighbourhood, where the People are *very ſtupid*, before ſhe can poſſibly paſs for a Witch.

'Twas a Saying of Mr. *Williams*, who would ſometimes be jocoſe, and had the Art of making even Satire
agreeable;

agreeable; that if ever *Jane* deserved the Character of a Witch, it was after th's Money was left her; for that with her five thousand Pounds, she did more Acts of Charity and friendly Offices, than all the People of Fortune within fifty Miles of the Place.

After this, Sir *William* inveighed against the absurd and foolish Notions, which the Country People had imbibed concerning Witches, and Witchcraft, and having proved that there was no such Thing, but that all were the Effects of Folly and Ignorance, he gave the Court such an Account of Mrs. *Margery*, and her Virtue, good Sense, and prudent Behaviour, that the Gentlemen present were enamoured with her, and returned her public Thanks for the great Service she had done the Country,

try; one Gentleman in particular,
I mean Sir *Charles Jones*, had conceived such an high Opinion of her,
that he offered her a considerable Sum
to take the Care of his Family, and
the Education of his Daughter, which,
however, she refused; but this Gentleman, sending for her afterwards
when he had a dangerous Fit of Ill-
ness, she went, and behaved so pru-
dently in the Family, and so tenderly
of him and his Daughter, that he
would not permit her to leave his
House, but soon after made her Pro-
posals of Marriage. She was truly
sensible of the Honour he intended
her, but though poor, she would not
consent to be made a Lady, 'till he
had effectually provided for his
Daughter: For she told him, that
Power was a dangerous Thing to be
trusted with, and that a good Man

α

ur Woman would never throw themselves into the Road of Temptation.

All Things being settled, and the
Day fixed, the Neighbours came in
Crouds to see the Wedding; for they
were all glad, that one who had been
such a good little Girl, and was become such a virtuous and good Woman, was going to be made a Lady;
but just as the Clergyman had opened
his Book, a Gentleman richly dressed

I   ran

ran into the Church, and cry'd, Stop!
stop! This greatly alarmed the Con-
gregation, particularly the intended Bride and Bridegroom, whom he
first accosted, and desired to speak
with them apart. After they had
been talking some little Time, the
People were greatly surprized to see
Sir *Charles* stand Motionless, and his
Bride cry, and faint away in the
Stranger's Arms. This seeming Grief
however, was only a Prelude to a
Flood of Joy, which immediately
succeeded ; for you must know, gentle
Reader, that this Gentleman, so
richly dressed and bedizened with
Lace, was that identical little Boy,
whom you before saw in the Sailor's
Habit ; in short, it was little *Tom
Two-Shoes*, Mrs. *Margery's* Brother,
who was just come from beyond Sea,
where he had made a large Fortune,
and

and hearing, as soon as he landed, of his Sister's intended Wedding, had rode Post, to see that a proper Settlement was made on her; which he thought she was now intitled to, as he himself was both able and willing to give her an ample Fortune. They soon returned to the Communion-Table, and were married in Tears, but they were Tears of Joy.

There is something wonderful in this young Gentleman's Preservation and Success in Life; which we shall acquaint the Reader of, in the History of his Life and Adventures, which will soon be published.

I 2   CHAP.

C H A P. VII. and Laſt.

The true Uſe of Riches.

THE Harmony and Affection that
ſubſiſted between this happy
Couple, is inexpreſſible; but Time,
which diſſolves the cloſeſt Union,
after ſix Years, ſevered Sir *Charles*
from his Lady; for being ſeized with
a violent Fever he died, and left her
full of Grief, tho' poſſeſſed of a large
Fortune.

We forgot to remark, that after
her Marriage, *Lady Jones* (for ſo we
muſt now call her) ordered the Chappel to be fitted up, and allowed the
Chaplain a conſiderable Sum out of
her own private Purſe, to viſit the
Sick, and ſay Prayers every Day in
the Chappel to all the People that
could

could attend. She also gave Mr. *John-son* ten Guineas a Year, to preach a
Sermon annually, on the Neceſſity
and Duties of the Marriage State,
and on the Deceaſe of Sir *Charles*;
ſhe gave him ten more, to preach
yearly on the Subject of Death;
ſhe had put all the Pariſh into
Mourning for the Death of her Huſ-band; and to thoſe Men who attend-ed this yearly Service, ſhe gave
Harveſt Gloves, to their Wives
Shoes and Stockings, and to all the
Children little Books and Plumb-cakes: We muſt alſo obſerve, that
ſhe herſelf wove a Chaplet of Flowers,
and before the Service, placed it on
his Grave-ſtone; and a ſuitable
Pſalm was always ſung by the Con-gregation.

About this Time, ſhe heard that
Mr. *Smith* was oppreſſed by Sir *Ti-*

mothy Gripe, the Justice, and his
Friend *Grafpall*, who endeavoured to
deprive him of Part of his Tythes;
upon which she, in Conjunction with
her Brother, defended him, and the
Cause was tried in *Westminster-hall*,
where Mr. *Smith* gained a Verdict;
and it appearing that Sir *Timothy*
had behaved most scandalously, as a
Justice of the Peace, he was struck
off the List, and no longer permitted
to act in that Capacity. This was a
Cut to a Man of his imperious Disposition, and this was followed by
one yet more severe; for a Relation
of his who had an undoubted Right
to the *Mouldwell* Estate, finding that
it was possible to get the better at
Law of a rich Man, laid Claim to
it, brought his Action, and recovered the whole Manor of *Mouldwell*;
and being afterwards inclined to sell
it,

it, he, in Confideration of the Aid
Lady *Margery* had lent him during
his Diftrefs, made her the firft Offer,
and fhe purchafed the Whole, and
threw it into different Farms, that
the Poor might be no longer under
the Dominion of two over-grown
Men.

This was a great Mortification to
Sir *Timothy*, as well as to his Friend
Grafpall, who from this Time ex-
perienced nothing but Misfortunes,
and was in a few Years fo difpoffeff-
ed of his ill-gotten Wealth, that his
Family were reduced to feek Subfiftence from the Parifh, at which thofe
who had felt the Weight of his Iron
Hand rejoiced; but Lady *Margery*
defired, that his Children might be
treated with Care and Tendernefs;
for they, fays fhe, *are no Ways accountable for the Actions of their Father.*

I 4   At

At her first coming into Power, she took Care to gratify her old Friends, especially Mr. and Mrs. *Smith*, whose Family she made happy,----She paid great Regard to the Poor, made their Interest her own, and to induce them to come regularly to Church, she ordered a Loaf, or the Price of a Loaf, to be given to every one who would accept of it. This brought many of them to Church, who by Degrees learned their Duty, and then came on a more noble Principle. She also took Care to encourage Matrimony ; and in order to induce her Tenants and Neighbours to enter into that happy State, she always gave the young Couple something towards House-keeping ; and stood Godmother to all the Children in the Parish, whom she had in Parties, every *Sunday* Evening, to teach them their Catechism, and lecture them in Religion

ligion and Morality; after which she
treated them with a Supper, gave
them such Books as they wanted, and
then dispatched them with her Blessing. Nor did she forget them at her
Death, but left each a Legacy, as will
be seen among other charitable Do-
nations when we publish her Will,
which we may do in some future Volume. There is one Request however so singular, that we cannot help
taking some Notice of it in this Place,
which is, that of her giving so many
Acres of Land to be planted yearly with Potatoes, for all the Poor
of any Parish who would come and
fetch them for the Use of their Families; but if any took them to sell,
they were deprived of that Privilege
ever after. And these Roots were
planted and raised from the Rent
arising from a Farm which she had
assigned over for that Purpose. In
short,

short, she was a Mother to the Poor,
a Physician to the Sick, and a Friend
to all who were in Distress. Her Life
was the greatest Blessing, and her
Death the greatest Calamity that e-
ver was felt in the Neighbourhood.
A Monument, but without Inscrip-
tion, was erected to her Memory in the
Church-yard, over which the Poor as
they pass weep continually, so that
the Stone is ever bathed in Tears.

On this Occasion the following
Lines were spoken extempore by a
young Gentleman.

How vain the Tears that fall from you,
And here supply the Place of Dew?
How vain to weep the happy Dead,
Who now to heavenly Realms are fled?
Repine no more, your Plaints forbear,
And all prepare to meet them there.

The E N D.

APPENDIX.

Containing a LETTER *from the* PRINTER, *which he defires may be inferted.*

SIR,

I Have done with your Copy, fo you may return it to the *Vatican*, if you pleafe; and pray tell Mr. *Angelo* to brufh up the Cuts, that, in the next Edition, they may give us a good Impreffion.

The Forefight and Sagacity of Mrs. *Margery*'s Dog calls to my Mind a Circumftance, which happened when I was a Boy. Some Gentlemen in the Place where I lived had been hunting, and were got under a great Tree to fhelter themfelves from a Thunder Storm; when a Dog that always followed one of the Gentlemen leaped up his Horfe feveral times, and then ran away and barked. At laft, the Gentlemen all followed to fee what he would be at; and they were no fooner gone from the Tree, but it was fhivered in Pieces by Lightning! 'Tis remarkable, that as foon as they came from the Tree the Dog appeared to be very well fatisfied, and barked no more. The Gentleman after this always regarded the Dog as his Friend, treated him in his old

Age

Age with great Tenderness, and fed him
with Milk as long as he lived.

My old Master *Grierson* had also a Dog,
that ought to be mentioned with Regard;
for he used to set him up as a Pattern of
Sagacity and Prudence, not only to his
Journeymen, but to the whole Neighbours. This Dog had been taught a thousand Tricks, and among other Feats he
could dance, tumble, and drink Wine and
Punch till he was little better than mad.
It happened one Day, when the Men had
made him drunk with Liquor, and he was
capering about, that he fell into a large
Vessel of boiling Water. They soon got
him out, and he recovered; but he was
very much hurt, and being sensible, that
this Accident arose from his losing his
Senses by Drinking, he would never taste
any strong Liquors afterwards.---My old
Master, after relating this Story, and shew-
ing the Dog, used to address us thus, *Ah,
my Friends, had you but half the Sense of
this poor Dog here, you would never get
fuddled, and be Fools.*

I am, Sir, Your's, &c.

W. B.

The B O O K S usually read by the Scholars of Mrs. TWO SHOES, are these, and are sold at Mr. NEWBERY's, at the *Bible* and *Sun* in St. *Paul*'s Church-yard.

1. The *Christmas-Box*, Price 1d.
2. The History of *Giles Gingerbread*, 1d.
3. The *New-Year's-Gift*, 2d.
4. The *Easter-Gift*, 2d.
5. The *Whitsuntide-Gift*, 2d.
6. The *Twelfth-Day-Gift*, 1s.
7. The *Valentine's Gift*, 6d.
8. The FAIRING or *Golden Toy*, 6d.
9. The *Royal Battledore*, 2d.
10. The *Royal Primer*, 3d.
11. The *Pretty Play-Thing*, 3d.
12. The *Little Lottery-Book*, 3d.
13. The *Little Pretty Pocket-Book*, 6d.
14. The *Infant Tutor, or Pretty Little Spelling-Book*, 6d.
15. The *Pretty Book for Children*, 6d.
16. *Tom Trapwit's Art of being Merry and Wise*, 6d.
17. *Tom Trip's History of Birds and Beasts*, Price 6d.
18. *Food for the Mind, or a New Riddle Book*, 6d.

12. *Fables*

19. *Fables in Verse and Prose by Æsop, an:* *your old Friend Woglog*, 6d.

20. The *Holy Bible abridged*, 6d.

21. The *History of the Creation*, 6d.

22. *A new and noble History of England*, 6d.

23. *Philosophy for Children*, 6d.

24. *Philosophy of Tops and Balls*, 1s.

25. *Pretty Poems for Children* 3 *Foot high*, 6d

26. *Pretty Poems for Children* 6 *Foot high*, 1s

27. *Lilliputian Magazine,* or *Golden Library*, 1s.

28. *Short Histories for the Improvement of the Mind*, 1s.

29. The *New Testament*, adapted to the Capacities of Children, 1s.

30. The Life of our Blessed SAVIOUR, 1s.

31. The Lives of the Holy *Apostles* and *Evangelists*, 1s.

32. The Lives of the *Fathers* of the *Christian* Church for the first four Centuries, 1s.

33. A Concise *Exposition* of the Book of *Common Prayer*, with the Lives of its *Compilers*, 1s.

34. The *Museum* for Youth, 1s.

35. An Easy *Spelling Dictionary* for those who would write correctly, 1s.

36. A

36. A *Pocket Dictionary* for thofe who would know the precife Meaning of all the Words in the *Englifh* Language, 3s.

37. A Compendious Hiftory of *England*, 2s

38. The Prefent State of *Great Britain*, 2s.

39. A Little Book of Letters and Cards, to teach young Ladies and Gentlemen how to write to their Friends in a polite, eafy and elegant Manner, 1s.

40. The Gentleman and Lady's Key to *Polite Literature*; or, A *Compendious Dictionary* of Fabulous Hiftory, 2s.

41. The News-Readers Pocket-Book: or, A *Military Dictionary*, 2s.

42. A Curious Collection of Voyages, felected from the Writers of all Nations, 10 Vol. Pr. bound 1l.

43. A Curious Collection of Travels, felected from the Writers of all Nations, 10 Vol. Pr. bound 1l.

By the KING's Royal Patent,
Are Sold by J. NEWBERY, at the *Bible* and *Sun* in *St. Paul's Church-Yard.*

1. Dr. *James's Powders* for Fevers, the Small-Pox, Meafles, Colds, &c. 2s6d.

2. Dr. *Hooper's Female Pills*, 1s.
3. Mr. *Greenough's Tincture* for Teeth, 1s
4. *Ditto* for the Tooth-Ach, 1s.
5. *Stomachic Lozenges* for the Heart-burn, Cholic, Indigestion, &c. 1s. 6d.
6. The *Balsam of Health*, or, (as it is by some called) the Balsam of Life, 1s 6d
7. Dr. *Boerhaave's Purging Pills*, superior in Virtue to the *Scots* Pills, or any of the Aloetic Compositions, 1s.
8. The *Orignal Daffy's Elixir*, 1s. 3d.
9. Dr. *Anderson's Scots Pills*, 1s.
10. The *Original British Oil*, 1s.
11. *Pectoral Balsam* for Coughs, Asthmas, and other Disorders of the Lungs, 1s.
12. The *Alterative Pills*, which are a safe, and certain Cure for the King's Evil, and all Scrophulous Complaints, 5s. the Box, containing 40 Doses.——— *See a Dissertation on these Disorders sold at the Place above-mentioned,* Price 6d.

The Fairing

Preface

Commenting on John Newbery's reputation as a publisher of "purely entertaining" books for children, Sydney Roscoe allows him a total of "at least sixteen books in which the element of entertainment or recreation" predominates.[1] Nowhere in these sixteen books, however—not even among the riddles of *Food for the Mind* or the scatological verses of *The Museum for Young Gentlemen and Ladies*—is the voice of the preceptor entirely absent, but in *The Fairing* we surely find the one in which the most determined efforts are made to subdue him.

The book's very dedication is a hopeful sign. Such a sporting renunciation of the view that children should be seen and not heard bodes well for the casting out of yet more prohibitions and "You Know Who" has the reader on his side from the start. Furthermore, the clever play on the idea of "fairing" offers many imaginative possibilities. The *Oxford English*

iii

Dictionary tells us that the term, which means "a present given or brought from a fair," has been current since the late sixteenth century. By implying through the title page that this "golden toy" was just such a present, and by using "all the fun of the fair" as a theme for his compendium, "You Know Who" was astutely provoking appetites that would assure an eager market for his book. (Incidentally, it is also worth remarking that by 1764, the probable date of the book's first publication, the word "fairing" had gathered to itself the distinctive flavour of gingerbread and sweetmeats, cakes and custard, which are delights not wholly overlooked in the text that follows.)

So from the crackling exclamations of the opening pages, *The Fairing* stimulates the hope of a strange, new, careless vigour bursting into children's books with the hectic—if not altogether unforced—jocosity of the fairground itself. But it doesn't last, of course. Within a few paragraphs the trampling of foolish Dick Wilson gives warning of the imminence of a Lesson, and before long the fable of Honesty and Knavery has carried us into that quarter where, under Elizabeth Newbery's management, the Blossoms of Morality will soon have such abundant growth.

Nevertheless, the anonymous conductor of this fairground tour never seems to convince himself that golden toys should be weighted with lead, and his erratic progress towards a new freedom of expression gives *The Fairing* its abiding interest. Higgledy-piggledy with Dick Wilson, there is Sam Gooseberry from the Region of Nonsense with the news of Dick's "having twelve of his ten toes trod off"; twenty pages later we have no sooner seen off Miss Pride and Miss Prudence and virtuous old Cincinnatus than we are given an echo of "The House that Jack Built" and a rhyme about drunken Will that is on the brink of being a limerick. (Indeed, not the least reason for reprinting *The Fairing* is to show the amazing breadth of references that a children's book can contain: the Fieldingesque address to the Critic; the mention of Pompey the lap-dog, who was celebrated by Fielding's disciple Francis Coventry; the slightly adapted quotation from *Henry VIII* and the quotation from Young on page 35;[2] the rustic dialogue between Chopstick and Tumble-turf, where satire, with its motto,

v

PREFACE

"Money makes the mare to go," comes from a popular song;[3] and the scatter of proverbs and rhymes.[4] Most notable of all, of course, are the two complete tales: *Dick Whittington*, almost verbatim—apart from one or two interpolations by the fairground narrator—after the standard chapbook version, and *Puss-in-Boots*, a slightly simplified telling of Robert Samber's original translation of Perrault.*

Although it is unlikely that we shall ever be certain of the identity of "You Know Who," those sentimentalists who would like to attribute *The Fairing* to John Newbery himself must be allowed a considerable case. For just as this little compendium contains many references to contemporary writings and sayings, so too it incorporates references to other works from the same estimable publisher. Apart from the very typical advertisement on page 120 for "Mr Newbery's books"—with its note of Tom

---

*Puss-in-Boots is notable as an example of a fairy tale that could be seen to encourage all kinds of fraud and deception. It is therefore amusing to observe the teller's defence of his choice on moral grounds, even though he admits that "Fairy Tales should never be read but on Fair Days."

Trip and Jouler—there is also the inclusion of the theme of *Giles Gingerbread* in Chapter II (Giles's *Renowned History*[5] may have been published at the same time as *The Fairing*); the redeployment of traditional rhymes that had appeared in other anonymous Newbery publications (see note 4); while on page 50 there is a whole verse from *A Little Pretty Pocket-Book*, in which the lines on Leap-Frog have been adapted to the Up-and-down.

Whether such easy movement among the Newbery "house-material" argues Mr. Newbery himself as author, or whether it simply shows how well he organized his "editors," there can be no doubt that the conscious use of these references indicates the distinctiveness of "Newbery publishing." Appearing towards the end of the founder's busy life, *The Fairing* reflects many of the characteristics that were present in his earlier ventures. The prodigality of its woodcuts, the almost random whirl of events, the button-holing ease of its address, set it apart from the miscellanies or the variably sugared didactic pills of its competitors. For all the unsophisticated techniques of the time it has an air about it, a personality, which

PREFACE

demonstrates the potential influence of the publisher in the field of children's book production. As such, it both adds to and gains substance from its master's total *oeuvre*.

Brian Alderson

BRIAN ALDERSON has been concerned with children's books as a bookseller, student, reviewer, and parent for the last twenty years. At present he lectures on Children's Literature at the Polytechnic of North London School of Librarianship and serves as Children's Books Editor of The Times *newspaper.*

PREFACE

References:

1. Roscoe, S. *John Newbery and his Successors 1740-1814*. Wormley, Hertfordshire, 1973, p. 8.

2. Young, Edward. *Love of Fame, the Universal Passion. Satire I*. London 1725, ll. 171-4.

3. Given as from a collection of "Old Glees and Catches" in *Brewer's Dictionary of Phrase and Fable*. Eighth edition. London 1963, p. 584.

4. Iona and Peter Opie note *The Fairing* (along with *Little Goody Two-Shoes*) as the earliest juvenile sources for "Early to bed" and *The Fairing* as the second earliest printed source for "There was a little man" (*Oxford Dictionary of Nursery Rhymes*, Oxford 1951, pp. 127 and 291). It also appears to be the second main reference to "The House that Jack Built," the full rhyme first being given in Newbery's *Nurse Truelove's New-Year's Gift*, 1755 (Opie, op. cit., p. 231).

There are also two curious pre-echoes in *The Fairing*, the reference to the dog Keeper, a name which was to be widely popularized by E. A. Kendall in *Keeper's Travels in Search of his Master* (London: printed for Elizabeth Newbery, 1798); and a sentence that reminds one of a vastly greater piece of literature: "Time is to Eternity as this Grain of Sand to the whole World."

5. See Roscoe, op. cit., p. 200.

Selective Bibliography of Early Editions:

The Fairing: or, a Golden Toy; for Children of all sizes and denominations. London: J. Newbery, 1765 (first edition, known only by advertisements); "new edition," 1767 (only known copy imperfect); Newbery & Carnan, 1768; Carnan & Newbery, 1777; T. Carnan, 1780; W. Osborne & T. Griffin, 1782; T. Carnan, 1784; York: T. Wilson & R. Spence, 1805.

Tom Trip with old Ringwood and Jowler and Tray,
Is riding to Town for a Fairing...........Huzza!

THE
FAIRING:
OR, A
GOLDEN TOY;
FOR
CHILDREN
OF ALL
Sizes and Denominations.

In which they may see all the Fun of the Fair,
And at home be as happy as if they were there.

Adorned with Variety of CUTS, from
Original Drawings.

LONDON:

Printed for NEWBERY and CARNAN, at
No. 65, the North Side of St. Paul's
Church-yard, 1768.

Price SIX-PENCE bound and gilt.

TO THE

TRUE and GENUINE

LOVERS of NOISE,

This BOOK,

Which was calculated for their
Amusement, and written for
their Use,

Is most humbly inscribed

By

YOU KNOW WHO.

A 2

THE

PREFACE.

To the CRITICS *of the* Eighteenth
Century.

HA! ha! ha! ha! ha! Who do
I laugh at? Why at you, Mr.
Critic, who should I laugh at? A
Critic is like a *Currycomb*, and gives
Pleasure before he occasions Pain.

This Book you say is written without either Rule, or Method, or Rhyme,
or Reason. Pray, Sir, give me Leave
to ask you, What Rule is there for
Rioting? What Method is there in
Confusion? What Rhyme in a *Rattle-*
Trap?

Trap? Or what Reason in a *Round-a-bout?* Why none. And yet thefe are the Effentials of a Fair.

Sir, if I underftand the Matter, and, as Mr. Alderman *Bridle Goofe* fays, if I don't underftand it Nobody does. I fay, Sir, if I underftand the Matter (for we are now upon the Matter, and 'tis no Matter how foon we have done.) A Metaphor is a Kind of a Simile, and a Simile a Kind of Defcription, and a Defcription a Kind of Picture; and as all of them are intended to convey to the Mind an Image of the Things they reprefent; what they reprefent muft be like themfelves; and as this Book is a Metaphor, or Simile, or Defcription, or Picture of a Fair, it muft be like a Fair, and like nothing elfe; that is, it muft be one entire

A 3   Whole,

Whole, but a whole Heap of Confusion.

Sir, I am sure I am right. You may take my Word for it; and that will put an End to the Controversy; and I heartily wish all our Controversies about Nothing (which is indeed the Subject-matter of most Controversies) were determined in this Manner.

Pray, put this Book in the Front of your Library, and take Care you don't rub off the Gold on the Covers.

✤✤✤✤✤✤✤✤:✤✤✤✤✤✤✤

THE

FAIRING.

CHAP. I.

*Which begins in a Manner not prescribed
by the Ancients.*

HALLO Boys, hallo Boys.——
Huzza! Huzza! Huzza!

Come *Tom*, make Haste, for the
Fair is begun. See, here is *Jack
Pudding* with the Gridiron on his
Back, and all the Boys hallooing.

Make Hafte, make Hafte; but don't
get into the Crowd; for little Boys
are often trod upon, and even crufh-
ed to Death by mixing with the Mob.
If you would be fafe, my Dear, always avoid a Crowd. Look yonder,
Dick Wilfon there has done the
very Thing I cautioned you againft.
He is got into the Middle of that
great Mob. A filly Chit! That Boy
                                        is

is always thrusting his Nose into
Difficulties.   Surely, there never was
such an impertinent little Monkey.
How shall we get him out? See how
the Rogue scuffles and roars.

He deserves all the Squeezing he has,
because he will never take Advice,
and yet I am sorry for him. But what
comes here? Oh, this is Mr. Pug ri-
ding

ding upon a Man's Head, in order to
draw a Crowd together.

One Monkey makes many, fays the Pro-
verb, and, here it is verified.   See,
how the Rogue cracks Nuts,   and
throws the Shells at the People.   Who
tapped me on the Shoulder ? Oh, *Sam*,
what are you come puffing and blowing !

ing! Why you look as busy as a Fool
in a Fair.

Well, what News do you bring from
this Region of Nonsense? I have not
seen it, and should be glad to know
what is done, without the Trouble of
attending.

　　　　　　　CHAP.

CHAP. II.

Sam Gooseberry's *Account of the won-*
derful Things in the Fair.

WHY there is such a Mobbing
at the other Side of the Fair,
says *Sam*, as you never saw in your
Life, and one fat Fellow is got a-
mong them that has made me laugh
immoderately. Stand further, good
Folks, says he, what a Mob is here!
Who raked all this filthy Crowd together? Honest Friend, take away
your Elbow. What a beastly Crew
am I got among? What a Smell?
Oh, and such Squeezing. Why, you
over-grown Sloven, says a Footman,
that stood by, who makes half so
much Noise and Crowding as you!
reduce your own fat Paunch to a rea-
sonable

fonable Compafs, Sirrah, and there
will be Room enough for us all. Upon
this, the whole Company fet up a
Shout, and, crowding round my
Friend *Tunbelly*, left an Opening,
through which I made my Efcape,
and have brought off *Dick Wilfon*
with me, who, by being heartily
fqueezed, and having twelve of his
ten Toes trod off, is now cured of his
impertinent Curiofity. But you de-
fire an Account of the Fair, and I
mean to gratify you.

The firft Thing I faw, which gave
me Pleafure, was old *Gaffer Gingerbread*'s Stall, with little *Giles* behind
it. See him, fee him!

Here's Gingerbread, Gingerbread here of
    the beft;
Come buy all I have, and I'll give you
    the reft.

The

The Man of the World for Ginger-bread. What do you buy, what do you buy? ſays the old Gentleman; pleaſe to buy a Gingerbread Wife, Sir? Here is a very delicate one. Indeed, there is two much Gold upon the Noſe; but that is no Objeſction to thoſe who drive *Smithfield* Bargains, and marry their Wives by Weight. Will you pleaſe to have a Gingerbread

bread Hufband, Madam? I affure
you, you may have a worfe; or pleafe
to have a Watch, Madam? Here are
Watches for Belles, Beaux, Bucks and
Blockheads, who fquander away that
moft ineftimable of all Treafures *Time,*
and then cry for it. Pray read the
Motto to the Dial-plate, Madam;
you never faw a finer Dial-plate in
your Life, or a Motto that is more
fignificant, and that deferves fo much
of your ferious Confideration.

When Time is gone,
Eternity comes on.

Here, *Giles,* fpeak to it, fays the old
Gentleman.

Giles begins. This Watch, Madam, is only a Penny with all the
Gold about it. The Moral, Madam,

you

you have into the Bargain, which, if
righty underftood and properly applied, is of more Value than a thou-
fand Watches.

When Time is gone,
Eternity comes on.

Time is to Eternity, as this Grain of
Sand to the whole World; nay, it
is not fo much, yet we negleĉt and
fquander away that Time, which is
given us to fecure a glorious Eternity; which is in us the moft extreme
Folly and Madnefs. Let us think on
the Difference between living for ever
in Happinefs, or in Mifery, and we
fhall become better and happier even
in this Life; for it will always give us
extreme Pleafure to be affured, that
we have fecured to ourfelves Happinefs hereafter. This, Madam, is
fome Sort of Security even againft
                              Death,

Death,   Obferve what Cardinal *Wol-
fey* fays :

Farewel, a long farewel to all my greatnefs !
This is the ftate of man ; to-day he puts forth
The tender leaves of hopes, to-morrow blof-
   foms.   [him ;
And bears his blufhing honours thick upon
The third day comes a froft, a killing froft ;
And when he thinks, good eafy man, full furely
His greatnefs is a ripening, nips his root ;
And then he falls, as I do. I have ventur'd,
Like little wanton boys, that fwim on bladders,
Thefe many fummers in a fea of glory ;
But far beyond my depth : my high blown
   pride   [left me
At length broke under me ; and now has
Weary, and old with fervice, to the mercy
Of a rude Stream that muft for ever hide me.
Vain pomp and glory of this world, I hate ye,
O ! had I ferv'd my God with half the zeal
I ferv'd my king, he would not in mine age
Have left me naked to mine enemies.

 At this Inftant the Father came up
with Battledores in his Hand. Thefe
    B   Gen-

Gentlemen, says he, are my Battledores, which are to be tyed to the Breast-Button, and worn as so many Monitors to the Head, and to the Heart. The first is to be worn by Men of all Denominations, as it contains Lessons of universal Utility.

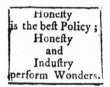

Honesty
is the best Policy;
Honesty
and
Industry
perform Wonders.

Speak to it, *Giles.*

Giles got up, and delivered the History of *Honesty* and *Knavery,* and of *Industry* and *Indolence,* as follows:

The

The HISTORY of
HONESTY and KNAVERY.

HONESTY and *Knavery* were both apprenticed in the same Town, to the same Trade, and being both out of their Time at the same Instant, they opened different Shops, and set up for themselves on the same Day. According to the Practice of Shop-keepers in the Country, they dealt in every Thing, even in Drapery, Grocery, Wine and Medicines. *Honesty* opened Shop in a decent Manner, bid his Customers welcome, sold them the best Goods he could buy for Money, at a moderate Profit, and would abate nothing of what he asked: But *Knavery* tricked up his Shop in a very gay Manner, fawned

upon

upon his Customers, bought such
Goods as he could afford to fell
cheap, and made frequent Abate-
ments, taking more or lefs, as he could
agree with his Customers. By this
Means he allured the Minds, and ftole
the Hearts of the People; fo that poor
Honefty had only the wife Men who
would deal with him, and thofe bore
no Proportion to the reft. Among
other Articles, they both dealt in
Wine, of which *Honefty* took Care to
procure the beft, even at any Price;
becaufe he knew, that the Health,
and indeed the Lives of his Customers,
depended much on the Quality, as
well as Quantity of what they drank;
but *Knavery* bought any ftummed
Stuff that he could get cheap, and,
to puff it off, hung out a fine large
Bufh. *Honefty* was advifed to do the
fame; but he only fhook his Head,
                                              and

and made this Anſwer, *Good Wine
needs no Buſh,* and ſo it happened ;
for many of the Cuſtomers who dealt
with *Knavery* died with the Stuff he
had given them to drink, whereas *Honeſty* loſt none of his Friends: They
grew heartier and better, while the
other were declining, which was ſoon
perceived; and the People all left
Knavery, notwithſtanding his fine Buſh,
and would deal only with *Honeſty.*
Thus by a ſteady Perſeverance, in doing what was prudent and juſt, and
without any Artifice whatſoever, he
gained the whole Trade to himſelf,
and did not leave *Knavery* one Cu-
ſtomer ; which ſo provoked him, who
was always an Enemy before, that in
the Night he broke open the Houſe of
Honeſty, and ſtole moſt of his Goods ;
but they were found upon him, and
he was tried and tranſported to a

B 3   Country

Country at a great Diſtance, from whence I hope he will never return to diſturb poor *Honeſty* again.

On this Circumſtance is founded the old and true Maxim, that *Good Wine needs no Buſh.*

To this Battledore *Giles* joined a *Gingerbread Paradox,* which here follows, with its Explanation.

PARADOX.

Induſtry and Indolence *were born on the ſame Day, and died on the ſame Day,* which was juſt at the Age of Sixty; *yet* Induſtry *lived fifteen Years longer than the other.* How can this be? Why, I'll tell you.

Induſtry, being a notable Fellow, made it a Rule to get up early every
Morning,

Morning, for he had learned this Maxim of his Father.

Early to Bed, and early to rife,
Is the Way to be healthy, wealthy,
*   and wife.*

So up he jumped at Six o'Clock, and sometimes sooner; but as for *Indolence,* he always lay in Bed till Noon, and when up, he found himself so weakened by laying long in Bed, that he had seldom Strength or Spirits to do any Bufinefs.

Now, as Sleep is a kind of Death, for, when fleeping, we have not the Use of our Reason, *Induftry* may with Truth be faid to have lived fix Hours a Day more than *Indolence,* which, in the Courfe of fixty Years, muft gain him fifteen: Befides this, he enjoyed good Healih; but *Indolence* was always fickly. *Induftry* gained a good Eftate
    B 4   from

from a small Beginning, and left all
his Relations and Friends Money to
make them happy; but *Indolence* idled
away a large one, which had been
gotten by his Father, and had at last
not enough to support himself. In
short, *Industry* died among a Circle of
his Friends, who really lamented his
Death, and buried him in a very decent Manner; but *Indolence* died in a
Ditch, and was buried by the Parish.
Idleness, saith *Solomon*, *will cloath a
Man with Rags*.

The next Battledore, says *Giles*, is
intended for the Ladies, and this is
the Lesson.

Pride *is a turbulent Companion, that
robs us of our Peace; but* Prudence
proves the Way to Happiness.

The

The HISTORY of

Miſs *Pride* and Miſs *Prudence.*

THERE was in the Country two Girls, called Miſs *Pride* and Miſs *Prudence.*

Miſs *Pride* was a pert tawdry Huſ- fey, who tricked herſelf up in all the Ribbons, Lace and Finery ſhe could get; but Miſs *Prudence* only dreſſed herſelf neat and decent. When thus furbelowed out, Miſs *Pride* toſſed up her Head with an inſolent Air, took no Notice of any one ſhe ſaw; and if ſhe had loſt her way, would rather go wrong, than aſk a common Perſon to ſet her right: Miſs *Prudence* too could hold up her Head, but then it was only to keep impertinent Fellows and Fools at a Diſtance; for to all

others

others she ever spoke cordially, *Good Night, Neighbour*; *Good Morning to you, Sir*; *How do you do, Madam?* and was very complaisant and obliging. Miss *Pride* was addressed by several Gentlemen in the Neighbourhood, and among others, by a Person of great Fortune and Accomplishments; but she gave herself such Airs, and made such a Fuss about Fortune and Settlement, Coaches and Card-money, that the Gentleman grew sick of her Affectation, and left her without taking his Leave, which was to her no little Mortification. After this, he addressed Miss *Prudence*, who behaved with Civility and Politeness, and told him, she had little Inclination to alter her Condition, but that she thought herself obliged to him for the good Opinion he had conceived of her. And when they came to treat about

Fortune

Fortune and Settlement, obferved
to him, that fhe fhould not be over
exact about thefe Things; for his
having the Character of a worthy
Man, weighed more with her than
all his Riches. In a little Time, Mifs
Prudence was married to this Gentleman of the firft Fortune and beft Ac-
complifhments in the Kingdom, which
fo ftung Mifs *Pride*, that fhe hated
Prudence ever after.

At this Inftant up buftled the old
Gentleman. Here, *Giles*, fays he,
take thefe Battledores for the Politicians. This is an Age of Politicks,
Boy ; even Tinkers are become *Ma-
chiavels*, and Coblers fettle the State
of the Nation. Read it, *Giles*.

The

The BATTLEDORE, *to be worn on the Breaſt Button of the Waiſtcoat next the Heart.*

I. No Title or Employment is honourable, which has not its foundation in Virtue.

II. In Caſes of Humanity and Mercy,
conſult your Heart; and in Caſes
of Juſtice, your Head.

III. Where the Public Weal is concerned, conſult your Underſtanding,
and if you have none, borrow.

IV. Serve your Friend, but conſider
yourſelf, and ſpare your Country.

V. When the Cauſe of your Country
calls you to Arms, ſhew your Cou-
rage, if you have any; but ſhew it
ſo that none may impeach your
Prudence.

VI. Are

VI. Are you a Man of Learning?
Shew it not so much by your Skill
in the *Roman* Language, as by a
Practice of the *Roman* Virtue.———
Their great Generals fought bravely
to sustain the public Glory, and
then retired to their own Ploughs,
to avoid an Increase of the Public
Expence.

On this Side the Gingerbread,
quoth *Giles,* you will observe, that
my Father has given you a curious
Picture of a Gentleman, with a Basket at his Back, coming from his
Fields, where he has been at Plough.

This

This is the famous and moſt truely
noble *Quintus Cincinnatus,* a brave
Roman, whoſe Actions are worthy of
the Attention and Imitation of every
Briton. This Man, at a Time when
the City of *Rome* was like to be de-
ſtroyed by the Diſſentions and Com-
motions of the People, was by the
Senate elected Conſul, and Meſſen-
gers

gers being difpatched for him to repair to *Rome,* and take on him that honourable and important Office, they found this illuftrious *Roman* meanly dreffed, and at Plough for the Subfiftence of his Family; for he had fold almoft all his Eftate to reimburfe thofe who had been bound for his Son, who was fled to *Hetruria.* The Meffengers faluted him by the Name of Conful, invefted him with the Purple, and with the Enfigns of Magiftracy, and then defired him to fet out for *Rome,* where his Prefence was greatly wanted; when, fo far was he from being lifted up by his new Dignity, or from the Thoughts of living grandly at the public Expence, that he paufed for a Time, and faid, with Tears in his eyes, *For this Year my poor little Field will be unfown, and we fhall be in Danger of being reduced to Want.*

Want. On his Arrival at *Rome*, he
reſtrained the Tribunes, ingratiated
himſelf with the Commons, and at
the Expiration of the Conſulate, returned to his rural Cot, and his laborious Life. But *Gracchus Clælius,*
exciting the *Æqui* and *Volſci* to re-
volt, greatly diſtreſſed the *Roman* Army; upon which *Cincinnatus* was cho-
ſen Dictator, and engaging *Clælius,*
he forced his whole Army to yield at
Diſcretion, and obliged them to paſs
under the Yoke, which was two Spears
ſet up, and a third laid acroſs in the
Form of a Gallows. After taking a
conſiderable Town from the Enemy,
he returned to *Rome,* with a more
magnificent Triumph than any which
had been before him. He then re-
ſigned his Office, and when the Senate and his Friends would have en-
riched him with the Public Lands,

Plunder

Plunder and Contributions, he nobly
refused them, and returned to his Hut
and his Plough.

The sensible Manner in which little *Giles* introduced these Stories,
drew all the People to his Father's
Stall, and among the rest the *Merry
Andrew.*

See here he is with his Hunch at his
Back. The Crowd that came with
him obliged us to leave the Place;
but just as we were going, *Giles* called

C   out,

out, Gentlemen, buy a House before you go. *'Tis better to buy than to build.* You have heard of the Cock that crowed in the Morn, that waked the Prieſt all ſhaven and ſhorn, that married the Man all tattered and torn, that kiſſed the Maiden all forlorn, that milked the Cow with a crumpled Horn, that toſſed the Dog, that worried the Cat, that killed the Rat, that eat the Malt, that lay in the Houſe that *Jack* built.

This is the Houſe that *Jack* built.

If there is any Part you do not like
you may eat it; and I sell it for a
Penny. Buy Gentlemen, buy and don't
build. How many of my Friends
have ruined themselves by building.
The unsufferable Folly of building a
fine House, has obliged many a Man
to lie in the Street. Observe what the
poet says on this Subject:

> *The Man who builds, and wants where-*
> *with to pay,*
> *Provides a Home, from which to run*
> *away.*
> *In* Britain *what is many a lordly Seat,*
> *But a Discharge in full for an Estate.*

A little further we saw one with the
Wheel of Fortune before him playing
with Children for Oranges. See here
he his again.

What do you say? Twenty may play
as well as one? Ay, and all may lose,
I suppose. Go away, Sirrah, what
do you teach Children to game?
Gaming is a scandalous Practice. The
Gamester, the Liar, the Thief, and the
Pickpocket, are first Cousins, and
ought all to be turned out of Company.

  You know little *Tom Simpson*, who
comes to our School? Poor Fellow, he
has scarcely a Shoe to his Foot, and
                                    would

would often go without a Dinner, if
he was not fed by the rest of the Boys,
who, to be sure, are very good to him,
as indeed they ought to be: For it is
our Duty to help those who are in Distress; whether we know them or not.
He that giveth unto the Poor, saith the
Wise Man, *lendeth unto the Lord; who
will in his good Time repay him seventy
fold.* This little Boy's Grandfather
was once the richest Man in all our
Country, beloved by his Neighbours, and happy in a Wife, and a
Number of fine Children, who were
all very good. Yet this Gentleman,
this Sir *William Simpson,* (my Father
used to shed Tears when he told the
Story) this Sir *William Simpson,* I say,
was ruined by a Set of Sharpers in
one Night. They first persuaded him
to play for small Sums, which they
let him win, then plied him with

Liquor till he was drunk, (how beaſtly and dangerous a Vice is Drunkenneſs!) and when he was in Liquor, they won Park after Park, and Farm after Farm, till they got his whole Eſtate, (What is bad enough for ſuch Villains?) He, poor Wretch, when he came to reflect on his Folly, and found that he had ruined his dear Wife and Children, ran mad, and was confined in *Bedlam*. Lady *Simpſon*, unable to ſupport herſelf under ſuch a Load of Misfortunes, died with Grief, and the Children, poor Babes, were all ſent to the Pariſh.

At this Inſtant up came *Dick Sudbury* crying. Here he is:

And

And what do you think he cries for ?
Why he has been at the Gaming-Ta-
ble, or, in other Words, at the Wheel
of Fortune, and loſt all the Money
that was given him by his Father and
Mother, and the Fairings that he received from Mr. *Long*, Mr. *Williams*,
and Mrs. *Goodenough*. At firſt he won
an Orange, put it in his Pocket, and
was pleaſed ; then he won a Knife,

C 4   whipt

whipt it up, and was happy; after this
he won many other Things, till at laſt
Fortune turned againſt him, as at one
Time or other ſhe always does againſt
thoſe who go to her Wheel and ſeek
her Favours, and he was chouſed of
all his Money, and brought nothing
away with him but a Half-penny
Jew's Harp. Why do you bellow ſo,
you Monkey? Go away, and learn
more Senſe for the future.

Would you be wealthy, honeſt Dick,
Ne'er ſeek Succeſs at Fortune's Wheel;
For ſhe does all her Votaries trick,
And you'll ſad Diſappointments feel.
For Wealth, in Virtue put your Truſt,
Be faithful, vigilant and juſt.

Never game, or if you do, never
play for Money. Avoid a Gameſter as
you would a mad Dog, or as you would
a Wolf that comes to devour you.

What do you juſtle me for? That
Fellow

Fellow is drunk now; see how he
staggers along; and how like a Fool
he looks! Drunkenness turns a Man
into a Beaft, and reduces him beneath
the Notice even of a Boy. Let us put
him in the Stocks; that was the Place
intended for those who barter their
Reason for a Pot of Beer, and waste
that which others want. In with him!
In with him!

See

See, here's drunken Will,
Who did nothing but swill,
Pray hiss at the Fool as you pass;
   He has spent all his Pence,
   He has lost all his Sense,
And is now dwindled down to an Ass.

Heyday! who comes here? Oh, this
is the Mountebank:

   He's come to cure ev'ry Sore,
   And make you twice as many more.

But hear him! hear his Speech, and
observe the *Merry Andrew.*

The DOCTOR'*s Speech.*

Gentlemen and Ladies, I am the Doctor of all Doctors, the great Doctor of Doctors, who can doctor you all. I eafe your Pains *gratis*, cure you for nothing, and fell you my Packets that you may never be fick again. [*Enter* Andrew *blowing; a fcrubbing Broom.*] Sirrah, where have you been this Morning?

Andrew. Been, Sir; why, I have been on my 'Travels, Sir, with my Knife, Sir; I have travelled all round this great Apple. Befides this, I have travelled through the Fair, Sir, and bought all thefe Gingerbread Books at a Man's Stall, who fells Learning by Weight and Meafure, Arithmetic by the Grofs, Geometry by the Square, and Phyfic and Philofophy by the Pound. So I bought the Philofophy,

lofophy, and left the Phyfic for you,
Mafter.

Doctor. Why, Sirrah, do you never
take Phyfic?

Andrew. Yes, Mafter, fometimes.

Doctor. What Sort do you take?

Andrew. Any Sort, no matter what
Sort; 'tis all one to me.

Doctor. And how do you take it?

Andrew. Why, I take it; I take it;
and put it up upon the Shelf: And
if I don't get well, I take it down a-
gain, and work it off with good Ale,
But you fhall hear me read in my
Golden Book, Mafter.

He that can dance with a Bag at his
Back,
Need fwallow no Phyfic, for none he
doth lack,

Again,

He who is healthy and chearful and cool,
Yet fquanders his Money on Phyfic's a Fool,
Fool Mafter, Fool Mafter, Fool, Fool.

Doctor. Sirrah, you Blockhead, I'll break your Head.

Andrew. What, for reading my Book, Master?

Doctor. No; for your Impudence, Sirrah. But come, good People, throw up your Handkerchiefs, you lose Time by attending to that blundering Booby, and by-and-by you'll be in a Hurry, and we shall not be able to serve you. Consider, Gentlemen and Ladies, in one of these Packets is deposited a curious Gold Ring, which the Purchaser, whoever he may happen to be, will have for a Shilling, together with all the Packet of Medicines; and every other Adventurer will have a Packet for one Shilling, which he may sell for ten Times that Sum.

Andrew. Master, Master, I'll tell you how to get this Ring, and a great deal of Money into the Bargain.

Doctor. How, Sirrah?

Andrew. Why, buy up all of them yourself, and you'll be sure of the Ring, and have the Packets to sell for ten Shillings a-piece.

Doctor. That's true; but you are covetous, Sirrah; you are covetous; and want to get Money.

Andrew. And, Master, I believe you don't want to get Physic.

Doctor. Yes, I do.

Andrew. Then 'tis to get rid of it. But,

> *He that can dance with a Bag at his Back,*
> *Need swallow no Physic, for none he doth lack.*

Huzza, hallo Boys, hallo Boys, hallo!

CHAP.

CHAP. III.

Sam Sensible's *Account of what he had seen in the Fair; particularly a Description of the* Up-and-down, *the North Country* Droll *and the* Puppet Shew.

IT is strange! but some Children will never take Advice, and are always running into Dangers and Difficulties. That Chit *Wat Wilful,* has been riding upon the *Up-and-down,* and is fallen off, and almost killed. You know what I mean by the *Up-and-Down?* It is a Horse in a Box; a Horse that flies in the Air, like that which the ancient Poets rode on. But here it is :

And

And here is poor *Wat*, and his Mo-
her lamenting over him.

Thefe

These lofty Flights are fit only for Poets and Politicians. If he had taken her Advice all had been well; for as he was going to mount, *Wat,* says she, don't be so ambitious. Ambitious People always tumble, when once up, it is not easy to get with Safety down. Remember what your poor Father used to read about Cardinal *Wolsey* and others, and don't think of mounting too high. But *Wilful* would, and so down he tumbled, and lies here a Warning-piece to the Obstinate and Ambitious. Had he taken his Mother's Advice, and rode upon the *Round-about,*

D

as *Dick Stamp*, and *Will Somers* do, he
might have whipped and spurred for
an Hour without doing any Mischief,
or receiving any Hurt. But he is a
proud obstinate silly Boy.

LINES on the *Up-and-down*, by a
        great Man at Court.

This sinks to the Ground,
While that rises high ;

But

But then you'll obſerve,
He'll ſink by and by :
Juſt ſo 'tis at Court,
To-day you're in Place,
To-morrow, perhaps,
You're quite in Diſgrace.

But I have ſeen at the farther End
of the Fair, *Tom,* a Droll, which, I
think, has good Senſe, and ſome
Knowledge of Mankind in it. The
Words are printed, and I have brought
them to you. Here they are :

The

The *Geography* of the *Mind*;

O R,

A *New Way* to know the *WORLD*.

Neighbour Tumble-turf, *and Neighbour*
Chopſtick.

Chopſtick. GOOD Morrow to you
Neighbour *Tumble-*
turf; pray, can you lend me your
Grey

Grey Mare to take a Ride *ſome* eight
or ten Miles to-day?

Tumble-turf. Why really, Goodman
Chopſtick, I am juſt going to carry
ſome Bags of Corn to the Mill to get
ground, for my Wife wants Flour
ſadly.

Chopſtick. There is no grinding
to-day, Neighbour; I heard *Cogg* the
Miller tell *Dick Hobſon,* that the Mill
was in Back Flood.

Tumble-turf. Say you ſo, Neighbour, I am ſorry for that. Then I
muſt ride to Town, and get my Wife
ſome Flour, or ſhe'll be out of all Patience.

Chopſtick. You need not do ſo,
Neighbour; I have got Flour enough,
and can lend you ſome Pecks of mine.

Tumble-turf. Your Flour may not
pleaſe my Wife, ſhe's very particular.

D 3 *Chop-*

Chopſtick. No Flour can pleaſe her ſo well ; why it was ground out of the laſt Corn I bought of you, which you ſaid was the beſt you ever had in your Life.

Tumble-turf. 'Twas ſpecial good, indeed, ſpecial good ! Neighbour *Chopſtick,* there is nobody ſo willing to lend as I am ; but my Mare does not eat Hay well, and I am afraid ſhe will not hold out.

Chopſtick. No matter for that, Neighbour ; I can get her two or three Feeds of Corn upon the Road.

Tumble-turf. Corn is very dear, Neighbour.

Chopſtick. That's true ; but when one is out upon Buſineſs it don't ſignify, you know.

Tumble-turf. It is a foggy Time, and my Mare has been hard worked, Neighbour; beſides, my Saddle is broke,

broke, and I have lent my Bridle.

Chopstick. It matters not ; I have a
Saddle and Bridle of my own.

Tumble-turf. But your Saddle will
not fit my Mare, Neighbour.

Chopstick. Then I can borrow of
Neighbour *Rogers.*

Tumble-turf. His is as bad as yours.

Chopstick. Then I can be fitted at
the *Squire's.* The Groom is an honest
Fellow.

Tumble-turf. Why, Neighbour *Chopstick,* there is nobody, you know, so
ready to lend as I am, and you should
have the Mare with all my Heart, but
she has got the Skin rubbed off her
Back as broad as my Hand.

Chopstick. I'll get the Groom to
stuff the Saddle. Nobody stuffs a
Saddle so well as *Dick Groom* ; the
poor Beast shan't be hurt.

D 4

Tumble-

Tumble-turf. Nobody is so willing to lend a Neighbour as I am, nobody so willing ; but my Mare is in rough Order, her Mane wants pulling sadly.

Chopstick. That is soon done, Neighbour ; I can do that myself, and *Dick Groom* will help me.

Tumble-turf. But now I think on't, she wants new Shoes.

Chopstick. There is Time enough for that ; the Days are of a good Length, the Mare trots well, and we have a Blacksmith at hand.

Tumble-turf. Aye, as you say, the Mare trots well, and the Days are of a likely Length both for Master and Man, but our Neighbour *Blacksmith* cannot shoe her easy. I always take her to Market, and get her shoed in Town by *Ned Hammerwell.* He shoes her to Pattern.

Chopstick.

Chopſtick. My Road lies through the Town ; it will be none out of the Way.

[*Enter* Tumble-turf's *Servant.*]

Tumble-turf. Here is Neighbour *Chopſtick* wants to borrow my Mate, *Tom,* prithee, ſtep, and ſee, if her Shoulder is not much wrung. [*Exit* Tom.] There is nobody ſo willing as I am to oblige a Neighbour when I can ; but [*Re-enter* Tom.]

Tom. Wrung ; aye, Maſter, ſhe is wrung indeed ; the Skin is rubbed off the poor Jade as broad as my Back : She is not fit to ride ; beſides, I pro-miſed her to Goodman *Ploughſhare* to fetch a Quarter of Coals. You know he has but two of his own, and if he can't have ours his muſt be idle.

Tumble-turf. Why indeed, Neigh-bour *Chopſtick*, I am ſorry it happens ſo. There is nobody ſo willing to

lend

lend as I am; and I wish I could let you have the Mare; but we cannot disappoint Goodman *Ploughshare*, for we owe him some Help. I am sorry it happens so.

Chopstick. I am sorry too; because it will be a Loss to both of us. You must know, Neighbour, I have had a Line from Sir *Thomas Wiseacre's* Steward, to come over directly. There is a Bargain of Timber to be sold, and if I miss, another Chapman may step between; which will be twenty Guineas out of your Way; for if I buy, you will have the Job of carrying it. I spoke about it. Sir *Thomas* pays well, and twenty Guineas is a good deal of Money, you know; but as the Mare is ill there is an End of the Matter.

Tumble-turf. Twenty Guineas, did you say?

Chopstick.

Chopſtick. Yes; twenty Guineas! But as the Mare is not fit to go, I muſt ſtay at home; and there is an End of the Matter, Neighbour.

Tumble-turf. Here *Tom,* tell Goodman *Ploughſhare,* that he cannot have the Mare to-day; for Neighbour *Chopſtick* wants her, and he muſt not be diſappointed. Another Day will do for him.

Chopſtick. But how can we manage about the Flour, and the Saddle and Bridle, and about getting her ſhod. Beſides, if the Mare is ill?

Tumble-turf. She is not ſo ill but ſhe will carry you very well. She eat her Hay well this Morning. As to the Flour, my Wife can ſtay ſome Days. I have a new Saddle and Bridle; you ſhall be welcome to them though they were never uſed. The Skin is not rubbed off broader than

my

my Finger ; and now I think on't,
she was new shod but Yesterday. She
will carry you well, Neighbour *Chopstick*, and I wish you a good Journey
and Success with all my Heart.

Chopstick. Thank you, Neighbour
Tumble-turf. A good Morning to
you.

*If you would borrow of a Friend,
That has nor will nor Heart to lend ;
Let his own Interest take the Lead,
His Interest best your Cause will plead ;
For, Sirs, it always happens so,
That Money makes the Mare to go.*

In the same Booth we were shewn
the comical Dogs and Monkies brought
from the Theatre in the *Haymarket*,
which were introduced with this short
Prologue :

Puppitt

Puppies and Coxcombs all draw near,
And Belles and Beaux, and Bucks come
    here;
Observe, the Feats perform'd by you,
The very Dogs and Monkies do.

The first Scene presented us with
two Monkies at Dinner dressed like
modern Beaux, and a third in a Li-
very waited on them at Table. See
here they are.

And

And they look as much like *Dick
Dapperwit* and *Jemmy Jeffemy*, as ever
you faw two Creatures in your Life;
but they bowed to the Company,
drank to each other, and behaved
better than moft of our modern Gentlemen.   Your Servant, Mr. *Pugg*.

We were then prefented with a
Grand Ball, which confifted of Dogs
and Monkies dreffed like Gentlemen
and Ladies, and they walked upon
their hind Legs, bowed, curtefied,
and danced Minuets, as is ufual in
Affemblies of the Polite.

The next Scene was made up of
feveral Dogs, that performed a Kind
of Harlequin Entertainment, which
was very droll, and conveyed to the
Spectators as much Knowledge as
Harlequin Entertainments ufually do.

We were then taught to ride the
Great Horfe, by a Monkey, which
was

was placed on a great Dog that was bitted and saddled, and pranced and performed all the Feats of a managed Horse.

Other Dogs then appeared walking on their hind Legs, dressed like Soldiers, with their Guns and Bayonets fixed, and ran up Ladders to storm a Castle, while the Guns were firing from the Top of the Works.

After this my old Friend the learned Dog made his Appearance. (See here he is.)

And he composed from the Letters
before him the following Poem.

The Dog on his own Abilities.

Let Pride no more your Hearts possess,
But here your Ignorance confess :
For sure, you all must blush to see
Yourselves exceeded thus by me.
   I for the Lawyers often write,
I for the Doctors oft indite ;
Billets I pen for Belles and Beaux,
And softest Sentiments disclose.
In Politics I oft engage,
And sometimes scribble for the Stage ;
Then cringe to get my Pieces on,
As all my Brother Bards have done.

After this he spelt all our Names, told
us the Time of the Day, and almost
told our Fortunes.

We

We were hurried from hence to
another Booth, and placed before a
Juggler with his Cups and Balls. See
here he is. *Quick, presto be gone.*

This conjuring Cur shewed us three
empty Cups and three Balls. The
Cups he turned down upon the Table,
and then taking the Balls and throwing them away, as he pretended, he
commanded the Balls under the Cup,

E   and

and on turning them up, lo they were
there. But *Dick Wilkins*, who you
know is a very arch sensible Boy, told
the Company there was no Mystery in
this; for there are four Balls, says he,
instead of three, one of which he con-
ceals between the two middle Fingers
of his right Hand, and by the Spring
of one Finger discharges it under the
Cup, when he puts it down. Then
taking another Ball to put into his left
Hand to throw away, as you would
imagine, he by rubbing his Thumb
conveys that also between his two
Fingers, and not into his left Hand,
and throws that under the Cup likewise; and having put one under each
Cup, he reserves the last Ball between
his two Fingers for the next Trick he
is to perform. Let me put down the
Cups, Master, says *Dick*, and then
try if you can command the Balls un-

der them. This the Man refused, and all the Company laughed at the little Fellow's Sagacity.

The next Trick he shewed was a Bag, in which Eggs were multiplied to a surprising Degree. First, the Bag was shewn empty, and then Eggs were found in it, and so on till a great Number were produced; and after they were all laid, as he pretended, out came a live Hen, to the Joy and Amazement of the Company.

This is a very pretty Trick, says *Dick*, and may make a Fool stare, but I will tell you how it is done, my Friend. You have two Bags that are made just alike; in one of the Bags there are many Foldings, and some Pockets in that Part of it next to you, in which the Eggs are concealed, and are dropped into the Bag as you would have them, through a Hole at the End

of

of the Pocket, which has Room e-
nough to admit of two Eggs paſſing.
In the other Bag you have concealed
a Hen; and when you pretend to
throw an Egg up to the Ceiling to
make it ſtick, you let drop that Bag,
and catch up the other juſt like it,
which hung on a Hook behind your
Table, and then let out the Hen. The
Man bluſhed, which was ſomewhat
extraordinary in a Juggler, and the
Company burſt into a Fit of Laugh-
ter.

After this, our Conjurer placed a
Die upon the Table, and deſired one
of the Company to throw it. A Lady
threw it, and up came Number *Five*.
This the Man covered with a leathern
Cap, and then aſking for a Groat's-
worth of Half-pence, he put them under the Table, and ordered them to
paſs through the Table, and remain
under

under the Cap. This done, he removed the Cap, and behold the Die
was gone, and the Half-pence there,
which was very surprising. He then
covered the Half-pence again with the
Cap, and commanded them again
thro' the Table, and we heard them
chink in his Hand. Then taking up
the Cap the Half-pence were gone, and
the Die there with the same Number
upwards, that was thrown by the Lady. This appeared very extraordinary, and our Juggler exulted a good
deal, saying, it could be done by no
other Cap, but that, which was *Fortunatus's* wishing Cap.

Say you so, says *Dick*; then listen
to me, and I will tell you how this
mighty Feat is performed. In the
first Place, my Friend, you get eight
Half-pence rivetted together, and then
cut a square Hole in the Middle thro'

E 3   all

all the Half-pence but the uppermost;
and this Machine, or Bundle of Half-
pence, you conceal in the little Cap.
Now, when the Die is thrown, you
cover it with the Cap, having these
Half-pence concealed under it, and
the square Hole that was made in
them admits the Die; so that the
Half-pence stand upon the Table.
Then taking those Half-pence, which
you borrowed, you rattle them under
the Table, and then lifting up the
Cap lightly, you discover those Half-
pence you had concealed there. When
putting on the Cap again, you rattle
the Half-pence you had borrowed under the Table, as if they dropped
through into your Hand, and squeezing the Cap with your Finger and
Thumb, so as to take up the Half-
pence rivetted together as well as the
Cap, you leave the Die with the same
Number

Number upward which had been thrown; and no Wonder, for the Die has never once been moved, but has all the Time stood in the same Place.

The Man was so confounded at this Discovery, that he would shew no more Tricks; and all the Company laughed to find, that our little Philosopher had more Wit than the Conjurer.

From hence we went to see the Puppet Show, and that impudent Rogue *Punch,* who came in, *Caw, waw, waw,* strutting and prancing, and turned his Backside to all the fine Ladies, as you may see.

E 4. I have

I have got, says he, I have got.
What have you got, cried the Fidler?
Why, I have got a Present for a
naughty Boy, says he, and held up a
Rod.

This brazen-faced Fellow, however,
was soon sent out to make Room for
Mr. *Whittington* and his Cat; of whom
we shall give you some Account.

Dick Whittington was a very little
little

little Boy, when his Father and Mother died; so little indeed, that he never knew them, nor the Place where he was born. He strolled about the Country as ragged as a Colt, till he met with a Waggoner who was going to *London,* and who gave him Leave to walk all the Way by the Side of his Waggon, without paying any Thing for his Passage; which obliged little *Whittington* very much, as he wanted to see *London* sadly; for he had heard that the Streets were paved with Gold, and he was willing to get a Bushel of it. But, how great was his Disappointment, poor Boy, when he saw the Streets covered with Dirt instead of Gold, and found himself in a strange Place without Food, without Friends, and without Money.

Though the Waggoner was so charitable, as to let him walk up by the

Side

Side of his Waggon for nothing, he
took Care not to know him when he
came to Town, and the poor Boy
was, in a little Time, so cold and so
hungry, that he wished himself in a
good Kitchen, and by a warm Fire in
the Country. In this Distress he asked
Charity of several People, and one
of them bid him, *Go work for an idle
Rogue.* That I will, says *Whittington*, with all my Heart. I will work
for you, if you will let me. The Man,
who thought this favoured of Wit and
Impertinence (though the poor Lad
intended only to shew his Readiness
to work) gave him a Blow with a Stick,
which broke his Head, so that the
Blood ran down. In this Situation,
and fainting for Want of Food, he
laid himself down at the Door of one
Mr. *Fitzwarren*, a Merchant, where
the Cook saw him, and being an ill-
natured

natured Huſſey, ordered him to go
about his Buſineſs, or ſhe would ſcald
him. At this Time Mr. *Fitzwarren*
came from the Exchange, and began
alſo to ſcold at the poor Boy, bidding
him go to work.

Whittington anſwered, that he ſhould
be glad to work, if any Body would
employ him, and that he ſhould be
able if he could get ſome Victuals to
eat ;

eat ; but he had had nothing for three Days, and he was a poor Country Boy, and knew nobody, and nobody would employ him. He then endeavoured to get up, but was so very weak that he fell down again, which excited so much Compassion in the Merchant, that he ordered the Servants to take him in, and give him some Meat and Drink, and let him help the Cook do any dirty Work that she had to set him about. People are too apt to reproach those who beg with being idle ; but give themselves no Concern to put them in a Way of getting Business to do, or considering whether they are able to do it ; which is not Charity. I remember a Circumstance of this Sort, which Sir *William Thompson* told my Father with Tears in his Eyes, and it is so affecting, that I shall never forget it.

When

When Sir *William* was in the Plantations Abroad, one of his Friends told him he had an indented Servant whom he had juſt bought, that was his Countryman, and a luſty Man, but he is ſo idle, ſays he, that I cannot get him to work. Ay, ſays Sir *William*, let me ſee him ; accordingly they walked out together, and found the Man ſitting on a Heap of Stones. Upon this, Sir *William*, after enquiring about his Country, aſked, why he did not go out to work ? I am not able, anſwered the Man. Not able, ſays Sir *William*, I am ſure you look very well, give him a few Stripes. Upon this, the Planter ſtruck him ſeveral times, but the poor Man ſtill kept his Seat. They then left him to look over the Plantation, exclaiming againſt his Obſtinacy all the Way they went. But how ſurpriſed were they, on their

Return,

Return, to find the poor Man fallen
off the Place where he had been fit-
ting, and dead. The Cruelty, says
Sir *William*, of my ordering the poor
Creature to be beaten while in the
Agonies of Death lies always next my
Heart. It is what I shall never forget,
and it will for ever prevent my judg-
ing rashly of People who appear in
Distress. How do we know what our
own Children may come to? The
Lord have Mercy upon the Poor, and
defend them from the Proud, the In-
considerate, and the Avaricious.

But we return to *Whittington*; who
would have lived happily in this worthy Family, had he not been bumped
about by the cross Cook, who must be
always roasting or basting, and when
the Spit was still, she employed her
Hands upon poor *Whittington*,

ill

till Mrs. *Alice,* his Master's Daughter,
was informed of it, and then she took
Compassion on the poor Boy, and made
the Servants treat him kindly.

Besides the Crossness of the Cook,
Whittington had another Difficulty to
get over before he could be happy,
He had, by Order of his Master, a
Flock Bed placed for him in the Gar-
ret, where there were such a Number

of

of Rats and Mice, that they often run over the poor Boy's Nose, and disturbed him in his Sleep. After some Time, however, a Gentleman, who came to his Master's House, gave *Whittington* a Penny for brushing his Shoes. This he put in his Pocket, being determined to lay it out to the best Advantage; and, the next Day, seeing a Woman in the Street with a Cat under her Arm, he ran up to her, to know the Price of it. The Woman, as the Cat was a good Mouser, asked a great deal of Money for it; but on *Whittington's* telling her, he had but a Penny in the World, and that he wanted a Cat *sadly*, she let him have it, and a fine Cat she is; pray look at her:

This

This Cat *Whittington* concealed in the Garret, for fear she should be beat about by his mortal Enemy the Cook, and here she soon killed or frighted away the Rats and Mice, so that the poor Boy could now sleep as sound as a Top.

Soon after this, the Merchant, who had a Ship ready to sail, called for all his Servants, as his Custom was, in

F   order

order that each of them might venture
some Thing to try their Luck; and
whatever they sent was to pay neither
Freight nor Custom; for he thought,
and thought justly, that God Almighty
would bless him the more for his Readiness to let the Poor partake of his
good Fortune; *He that giveth to the
Poor, lendeth to the Lord,* who will return it Seventy-fold.

All the Servants appeared but poor
Whittington, who having neither Money nor Goods, could not think of
sending any Thing to try his Luck;
but his good Friend Mrs. *Alice* thinking his Poverty kept him away, ordered him to be called, and here he
is,

she then offered to lay down some
Thing for him; but the Merchant
told his Daughter that would not do;
for it muſt be ſome Thing of his own.
Upon which poor *Whittington* ſaid, he
had nothing but a Cat, which he had
bought for a Penny, that was given
him. Fetch thy Cat, Boy, ſays the
Merchant, and ſend her. *Whittington*
brought poor Puſs, and delivered her

F 2

to the Captain with Tears in his Eyes, for he said, he should now be disturbed by the Rats and Mice as much as ever. All the Company laughed at the Oddity of the Adventure, and Mrs. *Alice*, who pitied the poor Boy, gave him something to buy him another Cat.

While Puss was beating the Billows at Sea, poor *Whittington* was severely beaten at home by his tyrannical Mistress the Cook, who used him so cruelly, and made such Game of him for sending his Cat to Sea, that at last the poor Boy determined to run away from his Place, and having packed up the few Things he had, he set out very early in the Morning on *Allhallows* Day. He travelled as far as *Holloway*, and there sat down on a Stone, now called *Whittington's-*

Stone, to confider what Courſe he
ſhould take ;

but while he was thus ruminating,
Bow Bells, of which there were then
only ſix, began to ring ; and he
thought their Sounds addreſſed him
in this Manner :

    Turn again Whittington,
      Lord Mayor of Great London.

Lord Mayor of London, ſaid he to
        himſelf,

himself, *what would one not endure to be Lord Mayor of* London, *and ride in such a fine Coach! Well, I'll go back again, and bear all the Pummelling and ill Usage of* Cicely, *rather than miss the Opportunity of being Lord Mayor.* So home he went, and happily got into the House, and about his Business, before Mrs. *Cicely* made her Appearance.

Here we must stop a little, to address the Children of six Feet high, and among them those formidable Heroes the Critics, whose awful Brows strike Terror into the Hearts of us little Authors.

Be it known then, to these Gentlemen, and to all the Knights of the Goose Quill, that we are not insensible of the Prescripts of *Apollo*, or ignorant of the Laws of the Drama. We know, that the Unities of Action, Time and Place, should be perserved as well in the Drama of *Whittington*,

as

as in thoſe of *Cæſar* or *Alexander*; but by your Permiſſion, Gentlemen, we muſt, in Imitation of ſome of our Poets, juſt ſtep abroad while you ſit upon the Bench, to let you know what has happened to the poor Cat; however, we are going no farther than the Coaſt of *Africa*, to that Coaſt where *Dido* expired for the Loſs of *Æneas*, and we ſhall be back with you preſently.

How perilous are Voyages at Sea, how uncertain the Winds and the Waves, and how many Accidents attend a naval Life !

The Ship, with the Cat on board, was long beating about at Sea, and at laſt by contrary Winds driven on a Part of the Coaſt of *Barbary*, which was inhabited by *Moors* unknown to the *Engliſh.* Theſe People received our Countrymen with Civility, and therefore the Captain, in order to trade with

them,

them, shewed them Patterns of the
Goods he had on board, and sent some
of them to the King of the Country,
who was so well pleased, that he sent
for the Captain and the Factor to his
Palace, which was about a Mile from
the Sea. Here they were placed according to the Custom of the Country,
on rich Carpets flowered with Gold
and Silver; and the King and Queen
being seated at the upper End of the
Room, Dinner was brought in, which
consisted of many Dishes; but no
sooner were the Dishes put down, but
an amazing Number of Rats and Mice
came from all Quarters, and devoured
all the Meat in an Instant. The Factor
in Surprise turned round to the No-
bles, and asked, If these Vermin were
not offensive? *Oh yes,* said they, very
offensive; and the King would give
Half his Treasure to be free of them;
for

for they not only deſtroy his Dinner, as you ſee, but they aſſault him in his Chamber, and even in Bed, ſo that he is obliged to be watched while he is ſleeping for fear of them.

The Factor jumped for Joy ; he remembered poor *Whittington* and his Cat, and told the King he had a Creature on board the Ship that would diſpatch all theſe Vermin immediately. The King's Heart heaved ſo high, at the Joy which this News gave him, that his Turbant dropped off his Head! Bring this Creature to me, ſays he, Vermin are dreadful in a Court, and if ſhe will perform what you ſay, I will load your Ship with Gold and Jewels in Exchange for her. The Factor, who knew his Buſineſs, took this Opportunity to ſet forth the Merits of Mrs. *Puſs.* He told his Majeſty, that it would be inconvenient

for

for him to art with her, as when she
was gone the Rats and Mice might
destroy the Goods in his Ship. But
that to oblige his Majesty he would
fetch her. Run, run, said the Queen,
I am impatient to see the dear Creature. Away flew the Factor, while
another Dinner was providing, and
returned with the Cat, just as the
Rats and Mice were devouring that
also. He immediately put down Mrs.
Puss, who killed great part of them,
and the rest ran away.

THE King rejoiced greatly to see his old Enemies destroyed by so small a Creature, and the Queen was highly pleased, and desired the Cat might be brought near, that she might look at her. Upon which the Factor called, *Pussey, Pussey, Pussey,* and she came to him; he then presented her to the Queen, who started back, and was afraid to touch a Creature, which had made such a Havock among the Rats and Mice; however, when the Factor stroaked the Cat, and cried *Pussey, Pussey, Pussey,* the Queen also touched her, and cried *Puttey, Puttey, Puttey,* for she had not learned *English.* He then put her down in the Queen's Lap, where she purring, played with her Majesty's Hand, and then sung herself to Sleep.

The King having seen the Exploits of Mrs. *Puss,* and being informed,

that

that she was with young, and would stock the whole Country, bargained with the Captain and Factor for the whole Ship's Cargo, and then gave them ten Times as much for the Cat as all the rest amounted to. With which, after taking Leave of their Majesties, and other great Personages at Court, they sailed with a fair Wind for *England*, whither we must now attend them.

> *The Morn ensuing from the Mountain*
> *Height,*
> *Had scarcely spread the Skies with Rosy*
> *Light;*

When Mr. *Fitzwarren* stole from the Bed of his beloved Wife, to count over the Cash and settle the Business of the Day.

He

He had but juſt entered the Compting-
Houſe, and ſeated himſelf at the Deſk,
when ſomebody came, Tap, tap, tap,
at the Door. Who's there, ſays Mr.
Fitzwarren? A Friend, anſwered the
other. What Friend can come at this
unſeaſonable Time, ſays Mr. *Fitzwarren?* A real Friend is never unſeaſonable, anſwered the other. I
come to bring you good News of the
good

good Ship *Unicorn*. The Merchant
buſtled up in ſuch a Hurry that he forgot his Gout ; he inſtantly opened the
Door, and who ſhould be ſeen waiting, but the Captain and Factor with
a Cabinet of Jewels, and Bill of La-
ding; for which the Merchant lifted
up his Eyes, and thanked Heaven for
ſending him ſuch a proſperous Voyage.
They then told him of the Adventures of the Cat, and ſhewed him the
Cabinet of Jewels, which they had
brought for Mr. *Whittington*. Upon
which, he cried out with great Earneſt-
neſs, but not in the moſt poetical
Manner,

Go, call him in, and tell him of his Fame,
And call him Mr. Whittington *by Name.*

It is not our Buſineſs to animadvert
upon theſe Lines. We are not Critics, but Hiſtorians. It is ſufficient
for us, that they are the Words of
Mr.

Mr. *Fitzwarren*; and though it is beside our Purpose, and perhaps not in our Power to prove him a good Poet, we shall soon convince the Reader that he was a good Man, which is a much better character; for when some, who were present, told him, that this Treasure was too much for such a poor Boy as *Whittington*, he said, *God forbid that I should deprive him of a Penny, it is all his own, and he shall have it to a Farthing.* He then ordered Mr. *Whittington* in, who was at this Time cleaning the Kitchen, and would have excused himself from going into the Parlour, saying, the Room was rubbed, and his Shoes were dirty and full of Hobnails. The Merchant, however, made him come in, and ordered a Chair to be set for him. Upon which, thinking they intended to make Sport of him, as had been too often the Case

in

in the Kitchen, he befought his Mafter not to mock a poor fimple Fellow, who intended them no Harm, but to let him go about his Bufinefs. The Merchant, taking him by the Hand, faid, indeed, Mr. *Whittington*, I am in earneft with you, and fent for you to congratulate you on your great Succefs. Your Cat has produced you more Money than I am worth in the World, and may you long enjoy it, and be happy. At length, being fhewn the Treafure, and convinced by them that all of it belonged to him, he fell upon his Knees, and thanked the AL-MIGHTY for his providential Care of fuch a poor miferable Creature. He then laid all the Treafure at his Mafter's Feet, who refufed to take any Part of it, but told him, he heartily rejoiced at his Profperity, and hoped the Wealth he had acquired would be

a Com-

a Comfort to him, and make him happy. He then applied to his Miftrefs,
and to his good Friend Mrs. *Alice,*
who likewife refufed to take any Part
of his Money, but told him, fhe really
rejoiced at his Succefs, and wifhed
him all imaginable Felicity. He then
gratified the Captain, Factor, and
Ship's Crew, for the Care they had
taken of his Cargo, and diftributed
Prefents to all the Servants in the
Houfe, not forgetting even his old E-
nemy the Cook, though fhe little de-
ferved it.

After this, Mr. *Fitzwarren* advifed
Mr. *Whittington* to fend for the necef-
fary People, and drefs himfelf like a
Gentleman, and made him the Offer
of his Houfe to live in till he could
provide himfelf with a better.

Now it come to pafs, that when Mr.
Whittington's Face was wafhed, his

G   Hair

Hair curled, his Hat cocked, and he was dreſſed in a rich Suit of Cloaths, that he turned out a genteel young Fellow ;

and as Wealth contributes much to give a Man Confidence, he, in a litt'e Time, dropped that ſheepiſh Behaviour, which was principally occaſioned by a Depreſſion of Spirits, and ſoon grew a ſprightly, and a good Companion ; inſomuch that Mrs. *Alice*, who had formerly ſeen him with

an

and Eye of Compaſſion, now viewed him with other Eyes ; which, perhaps, was in ſome meaſure occaſioned by his Readineſs to oblige her, and by continually making her Preſents of ſuch Things as he thought would be agreeable.

When the Father perceived they had this good Liking for each other, he propoſed a Match between them, to which both Parties chearfully conſented, and the Lord-Mayor, (See here he is.)　　G 5　　Court

Court of Aldermen, Sheriffs, the Company of Stationers, and a Number of eminent Merchants attended the Ceremony, and were elegantly treated at an Entertainment made for that Purpoſe.

History tells us, that they lived happily, and had ſeveral Children, that he was Sheriff of *London* in the Year 1340, and then Lord-Mayor;

that

that in the laſt Year of his Mayoralty
he entertained King *Henry* the Fifth
and his Queen, after his Conqueſt of
France. Upon which Occaſion, the
King, in Conſideration of *Whittington's* Merit, ſaid, *Never had Prince
ſuch a Subject*; which being told to
Whittington at the Table, he replied,
Never had Subject ſuch a King. He
conſtantly fed great Numbers of the
Poor. He built a Church and a College to it, with a yearly Allowance
for poor Scholars; and near it erected
an Hoſpital. He built *Newgate* for
Criminals, and gave liberally to St.
Bartholomew's Hoſpital, and to other
public Charities.

R E F L E C T I O N.

This Story of *Whittington* and his
Cat, and all the Misfortunes which
happened to that poor Boy, may be
conſidered as a Cure for Deſpair, as

G 3   it

it teaches us, that G O D Almighty has always something good in Store for those, who endure the Ills that befall them with Patience and Resignation.

This was a most extraordinary Cat, says *Dick Wilson*, but she was nothing to Puss in Boots. I'll tell you her Story.

PUSS IN BOOTS.

A Miller, who had three Children, left

left them no other Fortune than his
Mill, an Afs, and his Cat. The Di-
vifion was foon made. There was no
Occafion for a Lawyer. His Fees
would foon have confumed their little
Subftance. The eldeft had the Mill,
the fecond the Afs, and the youngeft
the Cat.

The laft was much concerned at
having fo poor a Lot. *My Brothers,*
faid he, *may gain an honeft Living by
joining their little Fortunes, but as for
me, when I have eaten my Cat, and
made me a Muff of her Skin, I muft die
with Hunger.* Pufs, who feemingly
fat unconcerned, heard him thus com-
plain, and with a grave and folemn
Look replied, don't be fo much concerned my good Mafter; you need
only give me a Bag, and get me a
pair of Boots, that I may fcamper
thro' the Dirt and the Brambles, and

G 4   you

you will see, that you have not so bad a Share as you imagine.

Though the Master of the Cat had but little Dependance on what he said, yet, as he had seen him perform so many cunning Tricks to catch Rats and Mice, as his hanging himself up by the Heels, and hiding himself in the Meal, pretending to be dead, he did not despair of his affording him some Assistance. When Puss had obtained what he asked, he booted himself like a little Man, and, throwing the Bag over his Shoulder like a School-boy, he held the Strings with his fore Paws, and ran to a Warren, in which were many Rabbits; he put some Bran and Sow-Thistles into his Bag, and stretching himself out as if he was dead, waited till some young Rabbits, unacquainted with the Deceits of the World,

World, came to examine the Bag,
and eat what he had put into it.

Scarce had he laid down, when a
young foolish Rabbit entered the Bag,
and Master Puss immediately drawing
the String, killed it without Mercy;
then proud of his Prey, went to the
Palace, and desired to speak with the
King.   Being admitted, he bowed to
his Majesty, saying, I have brought
you, Sir, a Rabbit, which my Lord
the Marquis of *Carabas* (for that was
the Title he was pleased to give his
Master) begs your Majesty to accept.
Tell thy Master, said the King, that
I thank him, and receive it with Pleasure.

Another Time he concealed himself
in the standing Corn, still holding his
Bag open, and when a Brace of Partridges ran into it, he drew the String
and took them both; after which he
went

went to prefent them to the King, as he had done the Rabbit. His Majefty alfo received the two Partridges with Pleafure, and ordered him fome Money to drink.

Thus Pufs continued two or three Months carrying his Majefty from Time to Time Game, which he pretended his Mafter had caught. One Day, when he knew the King was going to take an Airing along the Bank of the River, with his Daughter, the moft beautiful Princefs upon Earth, he faid to his Mafter, if you will follow my Advice, you will make your Fortune; you need only bathe in the River where I fhall fhew you, and leave the reft to me. The Marquis of *Carabas* followed his Cat's Advice, though he did not think it would be of any Advantage.

While he was bathing, the King
paffed

paſſed by, and Puſs began to cry with
all her Might, help, help, my Lord
Marquis of *Carabas* will be drowned.
At this the King looking out at the
Coach-Window, and knowing Puſs,
who had ſo often brought him Game,
ordered his Guards to run to the Aſ-
ſiſtance of my Lord the Marquis.

While they were pulling the poor
Marquis out of the River, Puſs coming
up to the Coach, told the King, that
while his Maſter was bathing ſome
Rogues had carried away his Cloaths,
though he had called out Thieves,
Thieves, as loud as he was able; but
the cunning Cat had only hid them
under a great Stone. The King inſtantly commanded the Officers of his
Wardrobe to run and fetch one of the
beſt Suits for my Lord the Marquis.

My Lord was no ſooner dreſſed
than waiting on the King, he was received

ceived in the moſt gracious Manner;
and as he was well made, very hand-
ſome, and the fine Cloaths ſet him off
to Advantage, the Princeſs was per-
fectly charmed with him; and the
King inſiſted on his ſtepping into the
Coach to take the Air with him.

The Cat, overjoyed at ſeeing his
Deſign thus happily begin to ſucceed,
ran before, and perceiving ſome Countrymen mowing a Meadow, ſaid, My
honeſt Lads, if you don't tell the
King, that the Meadow you are mowing belongs to the Marquis of *Carabas*, you ſhall be all cut as ſmall as
Herbs for the Pot. The King did not
fail aſking the Mowers, to whom the
Meadow belonged; when they all
cried to the Marquis of *Carabas*; for
they were ſadly afraid of the Cat.
Your Majeſty ſees, ſaid the Marquis,
that

that it never fails to produce a plentiful Crop.

Master Puſs, who kept running before, came up to ſome Reapers, and ſaid to them, My honeſt Lads, if you don't tell the King, that all this Corn belongs to my Lord the Marquis of *Carabas*, you ſhall be cut as ſmall as Herbs for the Pot. The King, who paſſed by a Moment after, was deſirous of knowing to whom all that Corn belonged, and aſking the Reapers, they all anſwered, may it pleaſe your Majeſty, it all belongs to my Lord the Marquis of *Carabas*. At which the King, addreſſing himſelf to the Marquis, expreſſed his Satisfaction, and complimented him on the Occaſion.

The Cat ſtill running before the Coach, gave the ſame Charge to all he met ; and the King was aſtoniſhed

at

at the great Estates belonging to my
Lord the Marquis of *Carabas.*

Puss at length came to a stately
Castle, which belonged to the richest
Oger that ever was known; for all
the Lands through which the King
had passed were his Property. The Cat,
who knew who this Oger was, and
what strange Things he could perform,
desired to speak with him, saying,
that he could not pass near his Palace
without

without doing himself the Honour of
paying his Respects to him. The
Oger received him with as much Civility as an Oger could, and made
him fit down. I have been assured,
said the Cat, that you have the Power
of assuming what Form you please,
and can transform yourself into a
Lion or an Elephant.   That is true,
returned the Oger, and to convince
you, I will become a Lion.   Puss was
so terrified at seeing a Lion before
him, that he crept into a Hole, but
not without great Difficulty, on account of his Boots : But on seeing the
Oger had resumed his natural Form,
he ventured out, and confessed that
he had been very much frightened. I
have been also assured, said the Cat,
that you have the Power of assuming
the Form of the smallest Animals,
and that you can change yourself into
a Mouse ;

a Mouse; but I must confess, that I think that impossible. Impossible! cried the Oger, see here, and instantly changing himself into a Mouse, skipped along the Floor. This the Cat no sooner perceived, than, springing upon him, he catched him in his Mouth and eat him up.

In the mean Time the King seeing the Oger's Palace, was resolved to go into it; and Puss, who heard the Rattling of the Coach over the Drawbridge, ran out, and said, your Majesty is welcome to the House of my Lord the Marquis of *Carabas.* How! my Lord, said the King, is this Palace also yours? Nothing can be finer than this Court, and the stately Buildings that surround it. If you please, we will walk into it. The Marquis presented his Hand to the Princess, and following the King, entered a

spacious

spacious Hall, where they found a magnificent Collation which the Oger had provided for his Friends; who were that Day to have paid him a Visit, but did not dare come, because the King was there. His Majesty was charmed with the good Qualities of the Marquis, and the Princess was violently in Love with him, which the King perceiving, and considering his great Wealth, said, after drinking five or six Glasses, I have such an Esteem for you, my Lord, that it shall be owing to yourself alone, if you are not my Son-in-law. The Marquis bowing very respectfully, accepted the Honour done him, and the same Day was married to the Princess; in consequence of which Puss became a great Lord, and never more ran after Mice, but for his Diversion.

H

As

As soon as *Dick* had finished this Story, *Sam Sensible* took him up with some Warmth. What, says he, do you intend to fob us off with a Fairy Tale, in which there is not the least Appearance of Probability? I don't consider, whether it is probable or not, says *Dick*, but I think my Puss is as good as your's; for in Matters of this Sort we are not so much concerned about the Truth of the Story, as the Moral it conveys; and tho' my Puss in Boots may be extravagant, she, in an indirect and pleasing Manner tells me, that a Man should not despair, because Fortune seems to frown on him; that a good Address and fine Cloaths captivates the Ladies; and that Flattery may catch a King and kill a Giant, as we see in the Case of the Oger. This calls to my Mind the Saying of *Diogenes*, who

being

being asked, what Beast was the most dangerous in case it was to bite one; answered, *If you mean the Bite of a wild Beast, it is that of a Slanderer; if of a tame one, it is that of a Flatterer.* All the Company laughed at the Defence *Dick* made for Mrs. Puss in Boots; but as her Story was so fantastical and out of Nature, Preference was given to the Cat of Mr. *Whittington*; and it was agreed, that Fairy Tales should never be read but on Fair Days, when People are inclined to have their Heads stuffed with Nonsense.

Here a great Noise in the Fair interrupted *Sam Sensible*, and cut the Thread of his Narration.

At this Instant up came two Ballad-singers; and see here they are.

H 2   *A*

A New LOVE SONG.
By the Poets of Great-Britain.
I.
There was a little Man,
Who woed a little Maid,
And he said, Little Maid, will you
wed, wed, wed?
I have little more to say,
So will you, aye or nay,
For the leaſt ſaid is ſooneſt amended,
ded, ded.

Then

II

Then replied the little Maid,
Little Sir, you've little said,
To induce a little Maid for to wed,
  wed, wed.
You muſt ſay a little more,
And produce a little Ore,
E'er I make a little Print in your Bed,
  Bed, Bed.

III.

Then the little Man reply'd,
If you'll be my little Bride,
I'll raiſe my Love Notes a little higher,
  higher, higher.
Tho' my Offers are not meet,
Yet my little Heart is great,
With the little God of Love all on
  Fire, Fire, Fire.

IV.

Then the little Maid reply'd,
Shou'd I be your little Bride,
Pray what muſt we have for to eat, eat,
  eat.　　H 3　　　　Will

Will the Flame that you're so rich in,
Light a Fire in the Kitchen,
Or the little God of Love turn the
Spit, Spit, Spit.

V.

Then the little Man he sigh'd,
And some say a little cry'd,
For his little Heart was big with Sor-
row, Sorrow, Sorrow.
I am your little Slave,
And if the Wealth I have
Be too little, little, little, we will bor-
row, borrow, borrow.

VI.

Then the little Man so gent,
Made the little Maid relent,
For to kill him with Love was a Sin,
Sin, Sin.
Tho' his Offers were but small,
She took his little All,
She could have but the Cat and her Skin,
Skin, Skin.

C H A P.

CHAP. IV.

Of Consequences: *Or, An Account of Things not to be accounted for, but from Experience.*

WHO made all that Noise just now? You don't know; no, I believe you don't, indeed. But, I will tell you. Why, it was *Tom Trip*, who beat *Woglog* the great Giant. He has got his Dog *Jouler* with him, and *Tinker*, and *Towser*, and *Rockwood*, and *Ringwood*, and *Rover*, all coupled together, and they draw him you see in a little Chariot. Here he comes; make Room, make Room for him! Your Servant, Mr. *Trip*; what brought you to Town, pray? Oh, you will not tell us, you say! Well; then I will tell these Gentlemen and

H 4 Ladies;

Ladies; for I think it may be of Use to them. Master *Trip*, you must know, will ride an hundred Miles at any Time to see any little Boy or Girl, who is remarkably good. He is the little Gentleman, who used to go round with Cakes and Custards to all the Boys and Girls, who had learned Mr. *Newbery*'s little Books, and were good; and having heard, that Master *Bill.*, and Miss *Kitty Smith*, were on a Visit at the Duke's, he is come a long Way to see them. Well, it seems very strange, that this little Boy and Girl should be so well beloved; that every Body should want to see them; but, if you consider how good they are, it will not seem strange at all. We are naturally fond of those that are good. Even naughty Children, who teaze others, love those best who are good-natured, and will

not

not teaze them. And so it is through
Life ; a Knave likes an honest Man
better than one of his own Stamp, and
would rather deal with him, because
he knows that the honest Man will
not deceive him. There was a Town
in some Country beyond the Sea,
where the People were so wicked as
to be all Thieves ; yet two *Englishmen,*
who were honest, went over, and lived
among them very well ; for as those
People were afraid to trust each other,
they all of them dealt with these two
Englishmen. However, they dealt with
them, not because they were *Englishmen,* but because they were honest
Men ; and they lived very well, and
got rich even among a Parcel of
Rogues. So true is that Copy in our
Writing-Books, which says, *Honesty is
the best Policy* ; and that other Copy,
which says, *Good Boys gain many
Friends,*

Friends, but naughty Boys none. If all
People were *good*, all would be *happy*;
and there would be no such Thing as
Fear in the World. We should have
no Occasion for Locks and Bolts, and
Bars, and Jails, and Whips and Rods;
and the Lawyers might burn all their
Books; for they would be useless.
But, I must run and see, how Master
Smith receives *Tommy Trip.* —— Stay
a little, and I will be with you pre-
sently.

CHAP. V.

Of Dress and Draggle-tails ; a Lesson
for GREAT CHILDREN.

WELL, there was great Joy at
their Meeting. Master *Smith*
embraced little *Trip,* and, then taking
him by the Hand, introduced him to
the young Marquis, who received him
very

very politely; that is, he received him
so as to make him happy; for the Business of Politeness is to make People
easy, happy, and agreeable. After
some Time, he led him to the Duke
and Duchess, who took great Notice
of him, I assure you: But at this Instant, an Adventure ensued, which
made us laugh heartily. And what
do you think it was? Why, as we
were then walking on the Green, a
Lady came up dressed in one of the
Sweep-street Gowns, which was held
up by the Duke's great Dog, *Keeper*.
See here he is.

This

This Lady flirted through the Company without speaking, and very familiarly brushed by the Duchess. Her Grace stood astonished, and the Duke was agreeably surprised, to see his favourite Dog *Keeper* so well employed. When this Lady stood still, the Dog ran to another, *bow, wow,* and took up her Train, and after that he took up the Trains of two Ladies at once; who, as they wanted to go different

Ways,

Ways, pulled, and could not think what was the Matter, and when they looked round and saw him, were frightened prodigiously, and called out for Help.

The whole Company soon gathered round, laughing; and the Extravagants, who wanted to bring this foolish Fashion into the Country, felt the Ridicule, and walked off the Green. Well! 'tis amazing, says the Duchess, that young Women should think to make themselves amiable by drawing six Yards of Silk in the Dirt after them. It is more amazing, answered the Duke, that Ladies should hope to get themselves good Husbands by Extravagance and Nastiness; for what can be more filthy than drawing their Negligees thus in the Dirt? But the Lass, continued the Duke, who has so agreeably ridiculed this foolish Fashion,

I must

I muſt be better acquainted with; ſo pray let her drink a Diſh of Tea with us at the Inn. A Card was immediately ſent, and Madam was introduced to her Grace, where ſhe behaved with ſo much Decorum, that the Company took her for a Perſon of Fortune; but when the Ducheſs had prevailed on her to throw off the Veil, who ſhould ſhe be but Mrs. *Dolly* the Dairy Maid, whom the young Marquiſs and Maſter *Smith* had engaged in this Scheme for the Benefit and Inſtruction of her Neighbours and fellow Servants; and had taught the Dog to ſupport her Train. The Ducheſs laughed immoderately at the Conceit, and gave her a new Suit of Cloaths; and the Duke ſaid, ſhe was a notable Baggage, and ordered her five Guineas. It is impoſſible to ſay how much the young Marquiſs and

Maſter

Master *Smith* were caressed on this
Occasion by the Duke, Duchess, and
indeed the whole Company; nor did
poor *Keeper* go without his Reward,
bow, wow, wow; for he had a good
Dinner ordered him, and was after
that frequently suffered to come into
the Parlour, till, in a Fit of Jealousy,
he pulled little *Pompey* out of a Lady's
Lap, and attempted to take his Place.
However, he soon recovered of this
Disgrace; for having been taught by
the Servants to fetch and carry, and
perceiving that the Duchess, when she
went out, had dropped her Watch,
he took it up, and brought it to her;
upon which she patted his Head, and
took him again into Favour.

There's

There's an honest Fellow for you!

After this, we were led to the Duke's House, where his Grace moralized on the Day's Diversion.

REFLECTION.

A Fair, says he, may be compared to a Journey through Life, where Mankind are always busy, but too frequently in Schemes that are idle and ridiculous. You now seem tired

of

of the Fair; and are all sensible, I hope, from the little Satisfaction these Baubles give you, that there is no real Pleasure, but in living a virtuous, peaceable and good Life.

Note, When *Keeper* had once learned his Business he would be employed; so that when Ladies came to the Duke's dressed in the modern Mode, the Dog always run to take up their Trains; upon which his Grace usually laughed, and said, his Dog was a great Enemy to Extravagance. We are told, that a noted Schemer took Advantage of this Circumstance, and bred a Number of Curs to support the Ladies Negligees at *Vauxhall* and *Ranelagh,* which he let out at a Shilling a Week, and their Board, and made much Money by it. But why so hard upon the Ladies, you'll say! Are not the Men in their Dress as whimsical

I   and

and ridiculous? Moſt undoubtedly.
It is not many Years ſince, ſome of
theſe Creatures put Wire or Iron Wigs
upon leaden Heads, and had their
borrowed Locks powdered with Blue,
inſtead of White, which Faſhion
would certainly have prevailed, if
Mrs. *Midnight,* at the little Theatre
in the *Haymarket,* had not dreſſed her
Raggamuffins in blue Perriwigs.

APPENDIX.

*Containing an Account of what was
done on the other Side of the* Fair.

WHILE we were thus enter-
tained with *Tommy Trip, Dolly,*
and the Dog *Keeper,* a Gentleman on
the other Side of the Fair had his
Pocket picked of his Watch, Pocket
Book, and a large Sum of Money. ——
How abſurd and fooliſh it is for People to carry any Thing that is valua-
ble into a Mob or a Fair, with them?
Thoſe

Thofe who are going where there is a
Crowd, fhould always leave their
Pocket-Books, Watches, and whatever is of great Value, at Home, and
take with them no more Money than
what they really want.

An odd Way of hiding Money.

Several Perfon: were taken up on
Sufpicion of picking the Gentleman's
Pccket, and among the reft a poor

Soldier

Soldier that came to beat up for Vo-
lunteers; who told the Mayor that he
was innocent, and that he had not
had a Farthing of Money in his Pockets for many Years. Upon this he
was searched, and several Pieces of
Silver being found upon him, the
Mayor was about to commit him;
but another Soldier stept up, and said
that Money was his. Yours, answered
the Mayor, how came your Money in
this Man's Pocket? Why, I will tell
your Worship, said the Soldier, this
Man here, who is my Comrade, loves
strong Beer so well, and Money so
little, that his Pay is always spent
before he gets it; and I can safely
say, that he has not seen Six-pence
of his own these seventeen Years;
which has been greatly to my Disad-
vantage; for as we were Chums, and
lay in the same Room, and sometimes
in

in the same Bed together, the Money
I put into my Pocket the over Night
was generally gone in the Morning,
and I was left pennyless and in want;
to prevent which, I have for some
Time past slipt my Money privately
into his Pocket, where it has lain very
securely and not been touched; for
tho' he has often searched my Pockets
for Money, I knew he would never
think of looking in his own.—The
Mayor laughed at the Conceit, and
the Man was discharged, but was di-
rected to behave himself better for the
future, and to keep his Fingers out
of his Friend's Pocket.

The Benefit of learning to Read well.

While they were searching after the
Gentleman's Watch and Pocket Book,
for which a great Reward was offered,
Miss *Sullen* and Miss *Meanwell* happened to go through the Fair; and the

I 3   first,

firſt, who was an obſtinate ill temper'd
Girl, and never would learn her Book,
picked up a Piece of Paper printed on
a Copper Plate, which ſhe looked at,
and then threw it in the Dirt, ſaying,
it was only a Bit of an old Almanack ;
for ſhe was ſo great a Dunce that ſhe
could not read it. This did not ſa-
tisfy Miſs *Meanwell*, who was as ſenſible and good-natured, as the other
was croſs and ignorant. She took the
Paper out of the Dirt, and on reading
it, found it was a Bank Note of twen-

ty Pounds; upon which she sent to
the Bell-man (See here he is)

to cry it, that the right Owner might
have it again, which you know was
very honest; and hearing that it had
been taken out of the Gentleman's
Pocket Book, who was now at the
Mayor's, and had got his Book a-
gain, she carried it to him; and told
him the Manner in which she got it;

I 4   and

and that she had sent the Bell-man to
cry it. The Gentleman was so pleased
with her prudent Behaviour, and in
particular with her Honesty, that he
gave her the Note for a Fairing. Only
think of that, twenty Pounds for a
Fairing! You see, *Honesty is the best
Policy*, as my Copy-book says. Had
she concealed this Note, and not ge-
nerously brought it to the right Owner,
and told the Truth, it would have
been taken from her in a disgraceful
Manner, and she would not have had
it for a Fairing. Twenty Pounds!
only think how many pretty Things a
young Lady may buy with *Twenty
Pounds*. She wished for a little Horse
to carry her Home; but the Mayor
would not let her lay out her Money
in that Manner, and the Gentleman
told her, as she was so good, and so
honest, and learned her Book so well,
she

ſhe ſhould go home in his Coach.

Miſs *Sullen* now put in for her Share, and ſaid indeed ſhe would have half; for ſhe found the Note firſt. Aye, ſays the Mayor, and was ſuch a Dunce you could not read it, but threw it down in the Dirt again. No, no, if ſuch a great Girl as you, who have been ſo long at School, can't read, you don't deſerve Fairings, or any Thing elſe. So pretty Miſs *Meanwell* had the whole, and the Coach to carry her home into the Bargain; and having bought a Parcel of little Books for her Brothers and Siſters, ſhe galloped away with the good News to her Father and Mother; who we may ſuppoſe kiſſed her a thouſand Times.

To

To a Good GIRL.

SO, pretty Miss *Prudence*, you're
come to the Fair;
And a very good Girl they tell me
you are.
Here, take this fine Orange, this
Watch, and this Knot;
You're welcome, my Dear, to all we
have got;
For a Girl that's so good, and so
pretty as you,
May have what she pleases——Your
Servant, Miss *Prue*.　　　　To

To a Naughty GIRL.

So, pert Miſtreſs *Prate-apace*, how came
    you here ?
There's nobody wants to ſee you at the Fair.
Not an Orange, an Apple, a Cake, or a
    Nut,
Will any one give to ſo ſaucy a Slut.
For ſuch naughty Girls we here have no
    Room,
You're proud, and ill-natur'd. —— Go
    Huſſey, go home.

Tu

To a Good BOY.

There was a good Boy who went to the
    Fair,
And the People rejoic'd becaufe he came
    there.
They all gave him Fairings, becaufe he
    was good,
And they let him have all the fine Things
    that he wou'd.
He went to the Puppet-fhow, then to the
    Play:
Make Room for the very good Boy there.
   ——Huzza.   To

To a Naughty BOY.

re was a bad Boy who rode to the
 Fair,
And all the Folks hiss'd becaufe he came
 there.
  They fent home his Horfe,
  Becaufe he was crofs.
Not a Thing could he get, of all he did
 lack,
And they laid his own Whip upon his
 own Back.

    Go home, Sarrah.
  The E N D.

The Holy Bible abridged, 6d.

Pretty Poems for Children 3 Feet high, 6d.

A New History of England, 6d.

The History of *Robinson Crusoe*, 6d.

Sixpennyworth of Wit, 6d.

The *Royal Psalter*, 9d.

The *Lilliputian Magazine*, 1s.

Pretty Poems for Children 6 feet high, 1s.

The *Museum*, 1s.

Short Histories, 1s.

The *Philosophy of Tops and Balls*, 1s.

The *New Testament*, 1s.

The Life of our SAVIOUR, 1s.

Lives of the *Apostles* and *Evangelists*, 1s.

Lives of the *Fathers*, 1s.

Exposition of the *Common-Prayer*, 1s.

The *Twelfth-Day Gift*, 1s.

The *Important Pocket Book*, 1s.

An Easy Spelling Dictionary, 1s.

Letters on all Occasions, 1s.

Words of the Wise, 1s.

History of the World to the Dissolution of the *Roman* Republic, 2 Vols. 1s. 6d.

A Compendious History of *England*, 2s.

An Account of the Constitution and Present State of *Great-Britain*, 2s.

A